An Elemental Meeting

The King's Weaver

Book Three

Novae Caelum

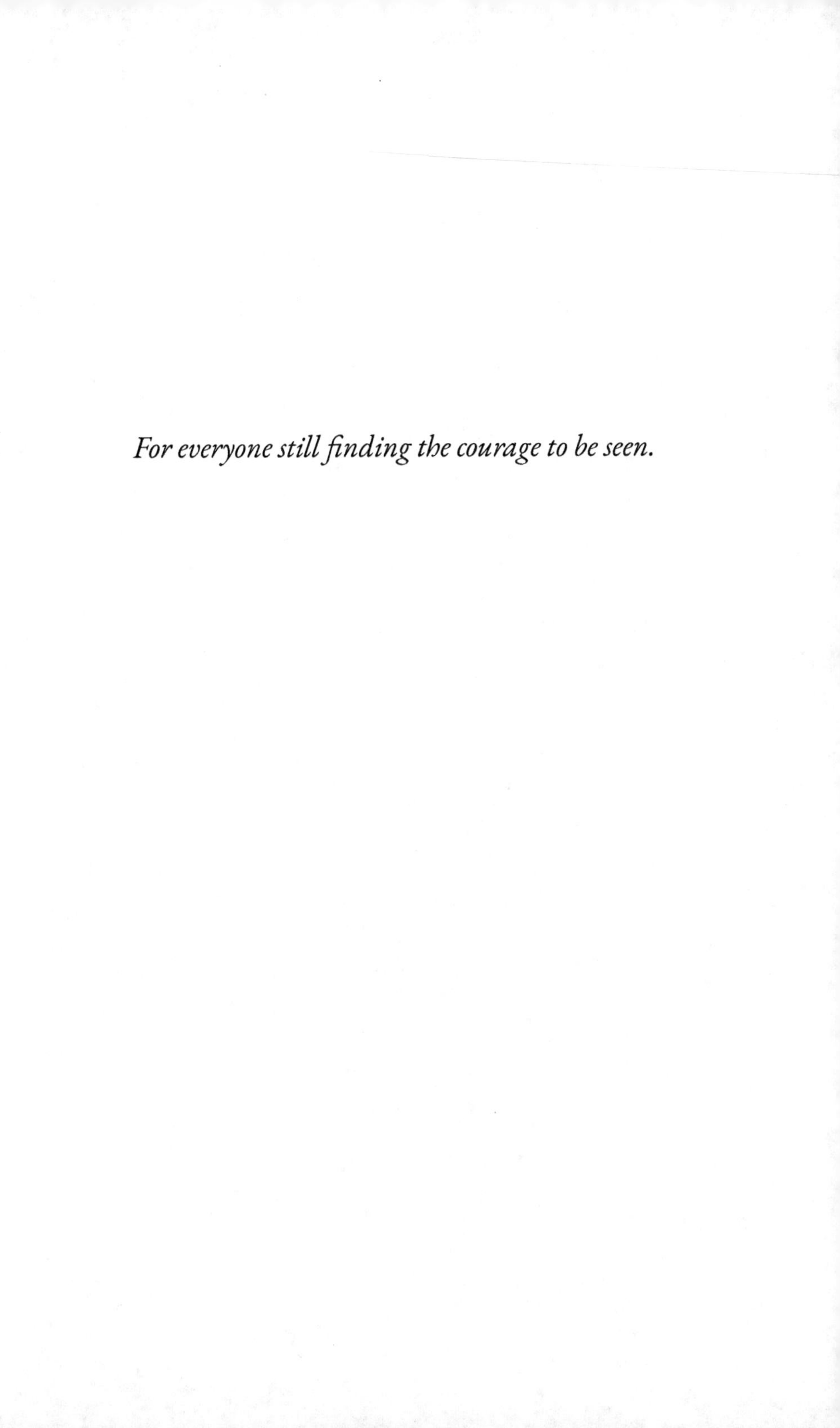

For everyone still finding the courage to be seen.

Author's Note

An Elemental Meeting came out of glorious nowhere, and I'm so glad it did! In preparing to write *An Elemental Husband*, which will follow Morgan, Valtair, and Elsira, I had to go back and write how Morgan and Valtair first met, seeing how they were making smexy-eyes frenemies glares at each other in *A Weaver's Heart*.

And that is this book. While it's novella length, I think it's vital to the series enough that I'm going to properly call it Book 3.

It wrenched my heart open and put it back a little more whole (even if their HEA is going to come in the next book, not this one!). I hope it brings you all the feels, too!

Note that this one has approximately two peppers of spice, still mostly non-descriptive. We'll call it a solid R.

CHAPTER 1

THE MEETING

VALTAIR

It's the kind of night no one should be outside in, the rain only stopping long enough to let me feel the chill. I hate traveling. Especially in the rain. *Especially* in the late autumn, when it all seeps into your bones until you swear you'll never be warm again.

I leave my carriage, and the cold follows me through the door of the inn.

Then the warmth hits—bodies pressed close, voices loud with drink, the smell of roasting mutton and wood smoke and wet wool. Nothing at all like the Barellan court. Nothing like the world I'm used to. Or my father's manor house I came from.

Maybe, tonight, that's a good thing.

And once I'm inside, rain drums again against the windows. At least it waited until I left my carriage.

I want wine. Forgetfulness, if I can find it.

Two days since my father's estate. Two days of his voice in my head: *You need to settle, son. Find someone suitable. Stop this wandering about.* As though my life is a problem to be solved with a ring and a marriage contract. He was the Minister of Finance for most of my life—but my life isn't a sum he can calculate and solve.

As though any of the men at court see me as more than a way into the favors of my father, and now that my father's retired, the king.

I told my father no.

Uh, loudly. And with great fervor.

I can still hear his shouts echoing off the stone walls of Valtair Manor.

But I'm here now.

I carefully pluck off my tight gloves, tuck them into my belt, stretching out my fingers from the ache.

The common room spreads before me, long tables crowded with travelers, the great hearth roaring at the far wall. Near the hearth, someone plucks a badly tuned lute.

I hope they're not going to try to sing. I already have a headache.

It should all be an ordinary inn. The kind of scene you see at any given inn on any given road.

But my attention catches on a man sitting alone in the corner, hunched over his ale. He looks like he is trying to fade into the background.

But he's staring straight at me with an intensity that I hadn't expected here.

He's young—my age, maybe—clean-shaven, his pale face pinked as he stares at me. His dark hair is messy, cut short and uneven, like someone took shears to it in haste. His clothes don't fit right. The shirt pulls across his shoulders, hangs loose in front of him. Borrowed, or bought without caring about the fit.

But it's not the clothes.

It's the tension in his frame. The way his shoulders curve inward.

The door opens behind me, and his eyes flick to the door, sharp and afraid, before he seems to take a breath and looks back at me.

As if I might actually be a point of safety in this inn from whatever he's running from.

Then the stranger's eyes widen and he blushes furiously, wrapping his hands back around his mug before hunching down further.

But he still looks up at me again. Checking I'm still here.

I look away to give him a little bit of space for dignity.

What's he running from? I know all about running.

He obviously recognizes me, but that's nothing new—everyone knows who I am at the Barellan court. I'm the son of the former Minister of Finance and the crown prince Torovan's best friend. Lord Thaddeus Valtair, notorious court rake. Now occupier of country inns.

He's not dressed like nobility, but something in his bearing, and the way he met my eyes, tells me he's not used to averting his gaze.

Nor should he have to be.

A short, balding man with a colorful apron appears at my elbow. The innkeeper?

"My lord! Welcome to our humble inn! We're honored—"

This man won't meet my eyes like the stranger just did, and now I'm unreasonably annoyed. Maybe it was foolish to think I could have even one night away from the cares of my social position and the Barellan Court.

"I need a room." My voice comes out rougher than I intend. I cough and try to smooth it. "Private. And wine. Top shelf, mind you. Or better yet, back room."

"Of course, of course." He's already bowing. "Our finest chamber for you, my lord. Fresh linens, good bed. And I'll send up a bottle from the southern valleys, excellent vintage—"

Better than the north. I don't want anything to remind me of my father's estate.

I count out coins without looking at them. More than the room costs, but I don't care.

"I'll eat down here."

His brows rise—nobility doesn't always sit in the common room—but he recovers. "The best table, then. By the fire—"

"That one." I nod toward a table with a clear view of the corner.

He hesitates, then snaps his fingers at a serving woman. I shrug out of my cloak, hang it near the door.

The serving woman clears the table, and I sit, stretching my legs under it. Which is a welcome relief after the cramped ride in the carriage. The fire's warmth finally starts to seep into my bones, but it doesn't touch the tightness in my chest.

I don't look at the corner. At the handsome stranger sitting in it.

But I'm aware. Of the way he shifts in his seat. Of the tension radiating from him even as he tries to project calm. Of his gaze sliding again toward me when he thinks I'm not watching.

The serving woman brings wine. I pour and take a long drink. It's decent—better than I expected from a roadside inn. The wine glass is cool in my palm, and the wine burns going down.

I still don't look.

But my awareness narrows to him. To the set of his shoulders, the nervous energy barely contained. The way he takes another sip, and I catch myself tracking the movement. Watching the line of his throat out of the corner of my eye. The way his hand tightens on the mug.

This is madness. I came here to forget. To blur the edges of the last three days until they stop cutting. I don't need this stranger who *obviously* comes with problems. He might think he's trying to blend in, but he looks like a storm of drama just waiting to happen.

The lute player starts something that might be a ballad and gods, yes, he is going to sing. Someone laughs too loud near the fire.

He doesn't move from his corner.

I don't move from my table.

When I let myself look again, he's already watching me. But he doesn't look away like someone caught staring. He just...watches. Like even though he doesn't want to be seen, he wants to be seen by *me.*

He holds my gaze for two seconds. Three.

Then he lowers his eyes with careful casualness, color rising again in his cheeks.

Heat crawls up my neck.

Gods, but he is handsome, in a delicate way that only emphasizes the noble bearing he's trying to hide. The bad haircut frames his round face in a roguish cast, only adding to the appeal. The way he holds himself shows confidence in his strength, though he's not by any means bulked out.

And he's interested. I know he's interested.

Is he worth dealing with whatever he's running from?

Or, is he flirting because he wants to play the games of the Barellan Court here? Am I just falling into another person who wants to use me for my connections?

My fingers tap against my glass. I should eat. Then go upstairs and let this night end. Maybe flag down the innkeeper again and tell him I'll eat upstairs.

The stranger's hunched over his mug again. His face is still flushed crimson.

And I have the sudden dizzying awareness that he's asking himself similar questions. Because yes, I know my reputation as a court rake. I do know. And usually, I don't care.

Yes, he's interested. But does he want to spend that interest on *me?*

And that...that short-circuits my better judgment. He knows who I am, and he's still hesitant. He's looked, but he hasn't made any moves to put himself in my good graces. Not anything like would happen at the court.

I carefully take a sip of my wine.

I haven't felt genuinely intrigued by someone in months. This pull. This spark of interest. And a hint of danger to spice it all up.

The serving woman brings food, and it almost feels like an interruption of intimacy. But I catch myself, tuck my napkin into my collar, and survey the meal in front of me. It's been long hours since I last ate on the road, and my mouth waters with the smell of it.

Roasted chicken, warm bread, cheese.

I glance at the man in the corner, and now he's not looking.

I look back at my meal on a wooden tray, then scoop up the tray and make my way over to him.

And now he's gripping the edge of the table, looking up at me with dismay.

I slow as I near his table. Did I misread the signals?

"Do you want company?" I ask. And waggle the tray.

His lips part. He's trim but not thin, but his eyes fixate on the meal like he hasn't eaten in a day.

I set it down and slip into a seat across from him at the table.

"I can't eat your meal," he says.

"Well, I can't eat it all alone."

Which is probably true. It's a large portion, and I have a waistline to maintain.

His mouth pulls tight. He looks around and leans in. "If you're trying to seduce me—"

I grin and sit back. "I was going to say the same. Those eyes you were making at me."

He flushes again, but keeps glaring at me.

I wave at the food. "Dig in. It's a gift, from a fellow traveler. And I didn't want to eat alone. The seduction is optional. But...on the table. If you want."

His lips twitch somewhere between a smile and a scowl, but he doesn't need any more coaxing to eat.

"Maybe," he says. And flicks up another look at me through thick lashes. While he turns bright crimson. Again.

Heat pools low in my belly. And gods but I'm losing all will to look away.

CHAPTER 2

FAMILY

MORGAN

He doesn't remember me.

Of course he doesn't.

I was sixteen. Wearing a dress my mother had commissioned for the Harvest Festival at the Barellan palace, the only time I can remember my family traveling the distance to attend.

I wore pale blue silk that made me look like a porcelain doll, and I hated it. My brown hair had been long then, pinned and curled into an elaborate style that took my maid an hour to arrange. I'd stood with the other daughters of high nobility while my mother introduced me to every eligible bachelor in the palace Great Hall.

Lord Valtair had been there with his father, Count Valtair. Handsome then, though younger. About the same age as me. I'd watched him all evening—the way his smile never reached his eyes when he spoke to the men presented to him, the way he slipped away to the wine table whenever he could, the way he laughed with the crown prince and the prince's twin sister. I saw his charm, but that was when he truly smiled.

I'd thought him beautiful and thought he'd seemed kind, though I overheard others talking about him with disdain. Warning the young men to never get involved, because he'd break their hearts.

It was jealousy, more like. Valtair's father was the Minister of Finance, and he'd grown up beside the crown prince.

And Valtair seemed completely uninterested in any of us beyond his court duties. Beyond his carefully calculated flirtations.

Even at sixteen, drowning in skirts I loathed with every fiber of my being, I'd recognized the performance of it. The careful distance.

My crush had been mild and impossible—he was a man who preferred men. And I thought I was a woman. I'd been told all my life I was a woman. That I'd grow up and marry to my family's advantage. That I'd do my duty.

That I'd never, *ever* get to be with anyone even remotely like Valtair.

So I forgot about my crush in my own years of slow and carefully calculated agony. Until I'd figured out why I was so unhappy.

Until I'd decided to do something about it and break free.

But I remember him.

And he has no idea who I am, I'm sure. He wouldn't be sitting here looking at me like that otherwise.

The relief cuts a sharp pain in my chest. And I cover it by biting into another piece of the chicken he offered.

I know I should be wary, that it will come at a price. But he's already said the seduction was negotiable.

And I've already said I might be interested anyway.

Why did I say that? Why, by all the gods, did I even hint at that, knowing I can never follow that through? And especially not with this man?

Why did I look at him at all? Why did I suddenly need to know what it felt like to be regarded by a man as a man?

Now he's sitting across from me, and I can barely breathe.

"It's good," I say into the silence, nodding at the food. I don't quite thank him, though I know I should. That feels like giving up a small bit of the ground between us.

The ground between us that is absolutely saturated in his cloying, expensive cologne—rose water and musk in quantities that would make a merchant blush. It's still the same scent he wore all those years ago, maybe his signature scent. I've never forgotten that scent.

Valtair makes a noncommittal noise around a mouthful. We were both famished, I know, so at least that's stalled the heart of this conversation for a few moments.

And given me time to better look at him up close.

He's beautiful. More than I remember, even. Coming into his prime has sharpened his features into something almost unbearable to look at—the sharp line of his jaw, the high angle of his cheekbones, the perfection of his warm brown skin that I wouldn't doubt takes hours of work to maintain. His hair is in dreadlocks now, the long locks pulled back with a filigreed gold clasp. Nothing overly fancy, but fancy enough.

He's dressed for travel, but his burgundy coat and dark green suede trousers fit his form exactly.

He's elegant and athletic, every one of his movements precise.

And he's watching me as he eats.

He's *here*. Looking at me. And I see his hunger, and it's not all from the food. Maybe even not mostly from the food.

He's looking at *me.*

That warms me all the way to a core I never thought would be warm again.

Or warm ever.

"So," he says, swallowing around a bite. "You're traveling alone?"

Not really a question.

I drain the last of my ale for one last bit of courage.

The coin purse in my pocket is nearly empty—I hadn't anticipated just how expensive inns would be. I'm going to need to find barns and haystacks to sleep in from now on.

But at least I'll have this meal.

And this moment with him to dream, if only for a moment, that my life had been different.

"I'm just passing through," I say.

He lifts one sculpted eyebrow.

"Passing through. In late autumn. In this gods-forsaken rain." His gaze drops to my hands—I pull them closer to me, taking another bite. I'm going to finish my portion of this meal. "Without proper provisions. Without a retinue. Without clothes that fit."

I swallow hard around a lump of meat and choke anyway, reaching for my mug of ale.

But it's gone. And I can't afford to get another.

Valtair frowns at me and hands me his wine. I'm coughing enough that I don't have much choice and take several sips, my eyes watering until my throat stops spasming and I get my food down.

He knows I'm born to nobility. And if I haven't fooled him with my simpler clothes, have I fooled anyone else?

I only stopped here to get something to drink and get out of the cold for a few hours. And maybe pretend to be drunk and slump over the table to get an hour of sleep in the warmth.

"I'm managing." I say. And take one last sip of his wine before handing it back. He takes the glass, eyes still on me.

"I'm sure." No mockery in his tone. It's almost... gentle. "But you're running from something. Or someone."

My throat tightens, and I grip the edge of the table, ready to push up.

I think I put at least some distance between myself and my brother pursuing me. I cut across the countryside when I saw him and his two retainers in the last town. If he's still following my same path south, he'll eventually have to double back along the other road. While I'm on this one.

Valtair leans forward. "Look, it's none of my business."

"No, it isn't," I say, not looking up at him as I choke down the last of my meal, ready at any minute to bolt.

He grips my hand, and I jerk my hand back. His brows crease, and he pulls away, sits back.

"I'm sorry," he says, and makes as if to stand. "I'll leave you to—"

"No."

And I'm suddenly terrified of losing what little familiarity he's brought to this moment.

He hesitates.

Regarding me with emotions I can't identify flickering across his face in the warm light of the inn.

"Please," I say. "Stay."

And I know I'm asking...more. So much more than I should.

But is it wrong to want a night with company when I've spent the last few nights in terror, trying to outrun a life that's no longer bearable to me?

He stiffens. I don't know what he sees in my face, but he says, "I'm not going to take advantage—"

I reach across the table and grip his wrist. "Valtair. You look like you need company, too."

His breath hitches when I say his name. He looks around us, as if trying to get his bearings again, then slowly sits down.

Takes a long breath. Looks at me.

He turns his palm up. "I had a fight with my father. It...didn't end well. I wouldn't mind a night of drowning out his absolutely infuriating voice in my head."

He punctuates that with another long sip of wine, then flags down the serving woman.

"Two more glasses, please. And"—he looks at me—" the bottle."

My pulse is picking up. I shouldn't have asked him back. Where this is headed is dangerous. Oh gods, but I know that.

But he's attracted to me, I know that, too.

And that feeling is the most electrifying thing I've ever felt in my life. The most dangerous.

What if I *want* it to go somewhere dangerous? Why can't I have something I want, for once in my life?

I'm exhausted. I've left everything I've ever had.

Why can't I have this one thing?

I know why I can't.

But still, I meet his gaze again as he turns back to me, and he smiles.

He told me his story. I owe him at least the surface of mine.

"I'm avoiding my family, too," I say. And I can tell by his slow nod that he knows that's hardly the whole of it, but he doesn't press.

"Family," he says, and takes the glasses that the serving woman brings back, and then the bottle.

His shoulders move in something between a shrug and a shiver.

I've heard his father, the Minister of Finance, is known as a humorless figure. But I can guess more from the defiant tension his shoulders settle back into.

"Which," he goes on, holding up his wine glass to inspect the dark liquid, "is why I mostly stick to the court. The people there are predictable. It's almost comical how predictable. All I need to do is play my part to survive."

What by all the gods does *he* need to survive? He's had

everything his whole life. Okay, maybe a strict father. But he grew up with the king's son, even. He's the son of a high minister. He can do anything he wants.

My family is noble, but not *that* kind of noble.

And I…will never be that kind of man.

I twitch as someone breaks out in laughter a table over.

And turn back to find Valtair's hand on mine again. Holding it more gently this time. And this time, I don't pull back.

"Why are you avoiding your family?" he asks. Then, very carefully, asks, "Are you in trouble?"

Like he would actually help a stranger if I was.

My eyes sting before I can think to marshal my control enough to stop them.

Valtair isn't who the court thinks he is. Anymore than I'm who my family thought I was, either.

"I—I can't be what they want."

He grunts, looks up at the ceiling, looking suddenly very tired. "Me either, friend. Me either."

Does he understand? How can he possibly understand?

No, he can't. Maybe recognize some similarities, but he's never had to flee from a life that would suffocate him. Has he?

"The difference," he says, looking back down again, not quite at me, talking into his wine, "is that I have the luxury of calling my running away a journey." He sighs. "But I'll never fully get away. My father might be retired, but he knows everything that goes on in the court. He'll expect a report that I'm back at court within days. Can't have his son gallivanting about the countryside, you know. There are appearances to maintain."

He says this in a tone that would have to resemble his father's.

"That sounds exhausting."

"It is." He looks at me then, and the directness of his gaze pins me in place. "So what do you think? Do you want to drown our woes and forget our families tonight?"

The air thickens between us.

I lick my lips, tasting the slightly too bitter wine.

Valtair's eyes drop to my mouth. Linger.

Rise again.

My pulse hammers in my throat.

"What's your name?" he asks. "You know my name. But I should at least know that if we—"

The door bangs open.

Cold air rushes in, the rain outside pounding even louder than the noise of the inn.

A new voice bellows from outside.

I know that voice.

My whole body locks up.

No.

My eyes snap to the entrance. Three men shake rain

from their cloaks—two retainers in my family's colors, and between them—

Timran.

My brother.

He's younger than me by two years, broader, his jaw harder. Meaner by far. His dark hair is slicked back messily from his face, wet from rain. He's travel-worn but well-dressed in expensive wool, good leather boots.

And he's searching the inn.

I duck my head. Turn toward the wall. Make myself smaller. My hand clamps on the wine glass until my knuckles go white. Blood roars in my ears.

Don't see me. Don't see me.

"What is it? Do you know them?"

Valtair's voice is quiet but urgent.

I can't look at him. Can't risk it.

"My brother," I manage, voice low and tight.

Valtair glances toward the door. Brief. Casual. But I see the tightness around his eyes, the thinning line of his lips.

"The one speaking to the innkeeper?"

"Yes."

Timran leans over the counter, his retainers flanking him. His voice carries authority even though I can't make out the words over the noise of the common room. But I know. I know what he's asking.

Have you seen a young woman, traveling alone? Dark hair, pale. Early twenties. She might be defiant or confused.

I heard him asking that of passers-by in the last town.

I know it will be something like that again. Something patronizing and *completely wrong.*

My throat closes.

"He does not look particularly friendly," Valtair says beneath his breath. At least we can't hear what Timran is asking. Timran lowered his voice just enough that we only hear the rumble.

I risk a glance at Valtair. He's watching me, not Timran. His sharp eyes assessing.

Then his expression clears, decision made.

"Come on." He stands smoothly, picking up his traveling bag and making his way around to my side of the table. He continues around me, positioning himself between me and the line of sight with my brother. "We'll hide you away for the night."

I stiffen and don't move, looking up at him.

When it was just flirting, when it was just locking eyes, the danger felt manageable.

But he's asking me to his room. And I don't know how much self-control I'm going to have. I haven't had much this night so far. And that...could lead to disaster.

Because I want him with a heat that's been pulsing in me since I saw him here. That's been driving me past all sense.

I want him to want me.

A pained look passes over Valtair's eyes.

"Gods, I'm not that much of a rake, despite my reputation, I swear on my soul."

I push up and hiss, "No, gods, I didn't think—"

But I'm used to seeing the world as a woman, too. Of seeing men as potential dangers, a very different danger than what I'm looking at now.

Or is it? What will he do if he finds I wasn't born a man?

How do I navigate this world of men? It's a different language, and one I should know, but I haven't yet learned to read even half of it. I've hardly learned how to speak it.

Valtair's head twitches to the side, but he doesn't look back at my brother.

And shit, yeah, we need to go.

"Lean into me," he says. "People don't pay attention to obnoxious couples."

I hesitate one precious second more, my heart pounding.

He isn't like the men I've known.

He doesn't know me. Doesn't owe me anything.

And maybe he wants a tumble, but he's made it clear he doesn't expect it, either.

He genuinely wants to help.

So I shoulder my own small bag, and take his hand.

His fingers close around mine, warm and sure, and for

a heartbeat we're frozen like that—connected, his grip solid, my pulse heavy under his thumb. Then he pulls me to my feet. I feel the controlled strength in it, the ease with which he moves.

His hand finds the small of my back. The touch burns through my shirt—his palm flat against me, fingers spread, guiding.

And for a moment I tense again—will he feel the binding garment? His hand is so close to the edge of it.

But he seems to sense my discomfort and lets go, taking my arm instead, like we're in court and he's about to present me to the king.

"Keep your head down," he murmurs, close enough that his breath brushes my ear and raises prickles down my neck. "Walk slowly. Don't run. Look a little drunk. Can you lean into me?"

I try, and the hairs on my arms stand on end again as I lean my head against his shoulder.

Gods, his cologne. Why does it smell atrocious and alluring all at once?

I almost stumble a step in my concentration to keep breathing, but his grip on my arm is steady.

Valtair waves down the serving woman. "I need my room key. And to know which room. Hurry." He caresses my hair and plants a kiss on my head, and I know it's for show, but my knees go weak with it.

With this insane mix of need and fear. I can still hear my brother talking with the innkeeper behind us.

The woman looks at the two of us, and I bury my face into Valtair's shoulder, throwing an arm around his neck. I steel myself and kiss the hollow of his neck.

His breath hitches, a ragged, shuddering sound.

"Hurry," he says again, his voice hoarse. And behind us, I hear a few hoots.

People *are* paying attention to us.

My heart kicks up again, and I keep my face turned into Valtair. He angles me away from the view of the bar.

I hear my brother's voice again, rising behind us, arguing about the price of ale.

"Here you go, my lord, it's room eight."

Valtair grabs the key and hurries us toward the stairs.

He slides his arm around my back again, and this time I don't care, I need the steadying.

I'm aware of every point of contact, the heat of him seeping through fabric and into my skin.

My pulse is pounding so hard I'm sure he can feel it against his hand.

And now the stairs take forever. I keep my face turned away, shoulders hunched, body angled.

The wood creaks under our weight.

My legs are water. My breath won't come right.

We round the landing.

And the common room disappears below us. The

noise fades, muffled by walls and distance. The hallway stretches ahead, lit by a single oil sconce down the hall, with doors on either side.

I no longer hear my brother's voice.

How did he find me here? Or is he just that determined to find me that he's already ridden on and doubled back? Did our father threaten him that he can't come back until he brings me home?

Our family needs the marriage they're trying to push me into.

But surely no one my brother asked could have told him about me, they would think I'm a man. My brother doesn't know I'm a man. And I have no intention of telling him, either.

Valtair pauses halfway down the hallway and turns to look at me. "Are you okay?"

I'm trembling. And my throat is so tight I'm not sure how I'm still breathing.

He pulls back further, and though the hall is dim, I see the concern in his eyes. "What did they do to you?"

I choke on something that I will not admit is a sob and brush past him, toward the door to room eight. I just need to get out of the open. I need safety, to know that my brother won't come up the stairs and find me here.

"It's nothing you think," I say. And it's not. No one has ever hit me, no one's ever laid a hand on me.

But there are expectations. And how do I explain how

dire it is that if I stay there, if I do my duty as the daughter of the house that they think I am, I will die?

It sounds dramatic to my own ears, though I know it's true.

I know.

Valtair follows. And when we both reach the room door, he pulls the key from his pocket. The metal scrapes in the lock. The door swings open.

He ushers me inside, and the door closes behind us with a soft click.

There's a banked fire in the small hearth and a single oil lamp on a tall dresser, mostly guttered. Valtair dumps his bag and moves toward it, turning up the light, then turns back to me.

Silence.

It's just the two of us now. In this private room. Alone.

The space is small but well-appointed. A sturdy bed with a plush mattress and clean linens. The hearth with a small bin of cut wood nearby. A washbasin on a stand. A window with actual glass, rain streaking down the outside in the moonlight. A table with a bottle of wine and two glasses waiting.

The kind of room someone with means stays in.

The kind I used to take for granted.

I was going to stay in the stables and hope not to get chased out.

My breath comes too fast. I press my hand to my chest, but my heart won't slow. The room spins—fear and wine and relief and terror all tangled together.

Safe. I'm safe?

Timran didn't see me.

Maybe I'm safe from Timran.

But I'm alone with Valtair.

In his room. With a bed. With the door closed and the night ahead and no one to interrupt or interfere or see.

I'm safe from my brother.

But standing here, feeling the heat of his arm still burning against my back even though he's no longer touching me, seeing the way his eyes track my face in the dim moonlight filtering through the window—

Seeing his concern. It's more than anyone has felt for me in a long while.

It's in the way he responded to me. The way he actually watched, the way he wanted to know how I felt. The protectiveness of his guiding me here.

The danger now isn't if he wants me.

The danger is that I want him, too.

The safety that he brings, and the night, as he said, of forgetfulness.

And that is a different kind of danger entirely.

CHAPTER 3

THE STRANGER

VALTAIR/MORGAN

VALTAIR

I watch him, this scared stranger, and wonder what I've gotten myself into. What family squabble I'm interrupting—though far be it from me to *not* get between an overbearing family and their overwrought son.

This looks like more than a squabble, though.

I listen for footsteps on the stairs. Voices in the hall. His brother's shout cutting through the night.

But I only hear the muffled sounds of voices and music from below.

"Then what did they do?" I ask again. Because I will not let his brother, who he obviously fears, get anywhere near him.

I'm not a fighter, and the brother...is not a small man.

But I have my connections at least. I can threaten with them. It's something. If the fool brother isn't such a fool that he would try to harm the son of Count Valtair.

But the stranger's shaking his head, looking like he's trying to regain his composure again, and mostly failing.

"Well, he can't reach you here," I say. "He can't search a private room that I paid for. And the bartender wouldn't let anyone search a room paid for by *me.*"

His lips twist with an ironic smile, and I don't know what that means.

And it hits me uneasily that I don't know him, I don't know what trouble he's in, and I don't know that he's being honest about it.

I've heard of nobles being robbed by clever schemes before.

But his fear...his fear is real. I'd swear it's real.

I move to the fire and stir it into more life. I feed it a small log, and light blooms, gold and warm.

When I glance back, he hasn't moved. His hands are fists at his sides.

"Sit." I wave at a chair beside the bed. "Please."

He hesitates, then takes it, sitting carefully, hunched in on himself. And I watch him try to compose himself again, deliberately sitting back, spreading his feet wider apart.

I light candles next—three on the mantle. The room fills with more soft, wavering light.

Better.

The wine bottle sits waiting. Southern valley wine again, if the innkeeper kept his word. I pour two glasses, carry one to my stranger.

"You look like you need a lot more of this."

His laugh comes out breathless. He takes the glass, but doesn't drink deeply. Not like he had before his brother came into the inn.

I'm jittering to know the ground I'm standing on with him and his family, but I don't press him. I don't think he'll let me.

And if the only distraction I get tonight is keeping him safe...well then, so be it.

I take my own glass and settle several feet away, near the end of the bed. He seems to need the distance.

After a few moments of sipping his glass and watching the fire, some of the tension bleeds from his shoulders.

"Thank you," he says quietly. "For helping me."

"Well, I'm not going to let a noble father ruin someone else's evening. If he was sent by your father?"

He makes a pained face. "Most likely."

The bitterness in my own words surprises me. Yes, I have issues with my father. Mostly *his* issues. But I don't usually let anyone know it, let alone a stranger.

And I've been pouring out my emotions all over the place tonight. Did my father truly rattle me that much?

The stranger leans forward. "So...you had a fight with

your father." Like he's desperate to get the subject back on me and off of him.

Well, okay.

"My exceedingly noble father explained to me a few days ago—at length and volume—just how much I need to settle down. Find a man that's suitable. Stop wandering about as though I have all the time in the world. And help maintain the family's reputation of 'solid-footing in the world.' Whatever the fuck that means." I drain half my glass. "Actually, no, I know what that means. He only wants me to pick from the list of high nobility of his choosing. And I can tell you right now, every one of those high noble sons is a godawful prick."

The stranger snorts.

"Except Torovan," I say, holding up a hand. "The crown prince is actually decent, though he's my friend, not my type. And there's me, I guess. Though I am still mostly a prick."

I watch the ghost of a smile come across his lips and revel in it.

"So you don't want to marry," he says, still watching the fire. And there's a knowing pain in that statement of fact.

"Ah. Did yours say the same? Is that what you're running away from? An unwanted marriage, or at least the threat that you'll have to have one?"

He shrugs, looking down. "Something like that."

I nod.

"No, I don't want someone *suitable*," I say again, and stretch my legs out, letting my head fall back to stare up at the ceiling. The room is fine enough, but there's a peeling old water stain up there. "I want someone who...who means something to me, you know? Not some court peacock who sees me as a stepping stone to the prince's favor. Or my father's. That's all they ever want."

And why do I think that this man, obviously noble but dressed in commoner's clothes, can understand that particular nuance? That feeling that everyone only sees me as a means to their ends, and not as actually...me?

He studies me. Not the calculated assessment of court, where everyone's trying to find weaknesses. It's something softer.

And what if it is understanding? How can this stranger possibly know the pain that's been slowly gnawing at me for years?

"Is that too much to hope for?" he asks, almost wistfully. "Someone to love you as you?"

I swallow hard and cover it with a shrug, tipping back my glass to drain the rest.

I shudder out a breath, trying hard to reset. This all is going into dangerously vulnerable territory.

"So, what is your name? I can't keep calling you 'the man I'm hiding from his family' in my head. Too many syllables."

A smile touches his mouth again, then fades. His jaw tightens, and he grips his own glass tightly.

"I'm…I'm Morgan."

Like he's handing me something precious. Breakable.

"Morgan." I test it. "I'm Valtair. Son of Count Valtair, in case you were wondering about the family dramatics."

"I know." His voice drops. "We met once. Years ago. At a Harvest Festival in the palace."

I pause, glass halfway to my mouth.

I would have remembered him. I'm sure I would have remembered him. I can't stop looking at the curve of his mouth, the way his lashes catch the firelight. The way his hair falls over his forehead. The way his hands are slowly kneading each other in his lap.

I would absolutely not have forgotten him, if I'd seen him at all.

The Harvest Festival. But there have been so many. With so many people at each one.

Faces blur together, every young man I've ever danced with. But I know I never danced with him.

I still have to ask: "Did we dance?"

"No," he says quickly, not meeting my eyes.

Oh, gods. What impression had I made on him? Some of my teenage years were not my best looks.

"Was I—" How do ask if I was an ass? "Was I pleasant?"

That smile again, fleeting. "You were kind. To everyone. Even when you clearly wanted to be anywhere else."

I go to take a celebratory gulp of wine, then finally push myself to get up and refill my glass.

"That sounds right. The festivals are all performance. Smile and nod and pretend you're enjoying yourself when really you're counting the minutes until you can escape."

I've learned to enjoy the Festival week in the last few years. Mostly. Or maybe make a show of tolerating it better.

"You did spend a lot of time at the wine tasting table," he says. "Not-not that I was watching. I just happened to see—"

The light is still dim, but I swear he's blushing again.

And I relax. Because no one this readable could ever be a thief.

"See?" I say, holding my glass up. "I'm at least consistent." I study him over the rim. "You still have me at a disadvantage. You've seen me at my most tedious, apparently. And I have no memory of you at all. And I'm sorry for that."

He flinches. Small, but I catch it. Why did he flinch at that? And now I'm wracking my memory for every awkward encounter that might have made that bad of an impression. Or did he think he was awkward to me?

I still can't place him.

"I wouldn't expect you to remember," he says.

MORGAN

Of course he still doesn't remember me. And I'm glad of it.

I'm *glad* of it.

I remember seeing him trim in his court clothes, his manner gracious even then, his hair braided back, his lips painted a light gold. I remember thinking that he might be someone I actually would like to dance with...until I overheard another young noble saying he only liked men.

And then I'd burned, because...well, I hadn't understood then why I'd burned.

I know now. When you grow up with layers of shame for who you are, you don't always see through them to your own reactions. Not right away.

If he remembered who I was then, he wouldn't be looking at me like this now.

And that is why this talking to him is dangerous.

Because it can't go any further than this. And he is being a perfect gentleman now, despite his reputation— and even I've heard of his court reputation, with my family as far from the palace as we are.

As *they* are.

They are not my family any longer.

"Okay, so," Valtair says, and leans forward, elbows on

his knees, glass dangling from long fingers. Firelight catches on his face, softening the sharp angles. Makes him look younger than his twenty-two or twenty-three, like me. "I'm asking because I want to know how to help you. Asking about your family, I mean."

I slowly rub my hands, just to have something to do with my hands.

I should keep deflecting. Should keep this surface-level and safe.

If I told my family I was a man, they might even be okay with it, on the surface.

The problem is, they've already planned my life out as a woman. They need me to marry, they need the connections that will bring. And if I'm a man, that just doesn't work the same way.

"So," he goes on, "you don't want to be what your family wants you to be."

"I can't." My voice cracks. I take a breath, try again. "It's not—I'm not stubborn, or rebellious, or anything like that."

Though that's all been hurled at me.

"It's that if I stay, if I do what they want, I'll—"

Die. Wither. Disappear into someone else's idea of who I should be.

"Suffocate," I finish.

His gaze holds mine. And there is actual understanding there. Real and deep.

That flares my temper again, like it did downstairs. Because how can he possibly know? Whatever he's dealing with, it's not what I'm dealing with.

"My father wants me to be an extension of him, too," he says. "A tool for maintaining his influence at court. Never mind what I want. Never mind that I spent my whole life being useful, and now that he's retired, he still wants to control me through his connections at court. Through Torovan, even. Do you know he wrote to Torovan and asked him to tell me I should stop wearing blue because he thinks it's not the right color for me? Whose father does that?"

I swallow. He means the crown prince. Because yes, he's best friends with the king's son.

"My father sees that friendship as leverage. Yes—okay, so, he sees Torovan as another son, too. But maybe that's just as bad. He wants to use *both* of us. It's just in his nature." He shudders.

"That's hardly fair to you," I say. Because it isn't.

Even if it isn't what I'm running from.

Or is it akin? Am I a son whose father's expectations are weighing me down, too, but he just doesn't know it yet?

"It's politics." Valtair takes another drink, then gets up to refill his wine glass again. "And now he's on me to settle down, to get married, and I told him no. Loudly. That marriage is not for me."

He stays at the dresser with his back turned to me, and I can see the tension rippling in his shoulders.

I take another drink of my own glass. I really need to pace myself, I doubt I hold wine as well as someone used to the court, like Valtair.

But I recognize that he's showing me something he rarely shows anyone. The side of him that isn't a court rake, but just...a man who's been worn down by the pressure of those who are supposed to love him.

"I left in the middle of the night," I hear myself say. "Took a horse, some supplies, and some clothes that didn't fit. I didn't leave a note. Just ran."

He turns back. "Where are you going?"

I shrug. "Somewhere...somewhere they won't find me. Somewhere safe. If anywhere is safe."

"I have to believe so." He downs his glass and pours more. "Otherwise what's the point of running?"

I watch him again, then finish off the rest of my glass.

Maybe I don't care if I won't hold my wine well.

Just now, it's taking the edge off.

"What do you want?" he asks suddenly. "From life. If you could have anything."

The question makes me blink, blooms a tight pain in my chest.

No one's ever asked me that. And it's the kind of question that would never come out without a few glasses between us.

"To be seen." The words escape before I can stop them. "Really seen. As who I am. Not who they see me as."

His expression softens. "That's not too much to ask."

"Isn't it?"

"No. Everyone deserves that."

The firelight flickers. Rain patters against the window. Somewhere downstairs, the common room noise continues—muffled laughter, the out of tune lute, voices rising and falling.

I listen.

My brother's voice?

No. Just the general din.

My hands tighten on the glass anyway.

"He won't find you, I promise." Valtair reads my tension. "Not tonight."

"You don't know that."

"No. But I'll make sure of it anyway."

The protectiveness in his voice does something to my ribs. Makes them tight, tighter than they should be in the binding garment. And damn that garment, I can't breathe.

"Why?" The question escapes. "Why are you helping me? You don't know me. You don't owe me anything. And I'm—I'm trouble."

He sets his glass down. And, near the hearth as he is, the light flickers softly against the earnest look in his eyes.

"Because I'd like to think if I ever needed to run, really run, someone would help me too."

My throat closes, and my eyes fill.

And maybe another man would turn away again at that, uncomfortable at the show of emotions.

But Valtair crosses to the bed again, sits a little closer this time.

"You're safe here, I really promise. Tonight, at least."

I believe him.

Maybe I still shouldn't. But I do.

"What do you want?" I ask, echoing his question. "From life."

He lets out a long breath, hunches as he stretches his back. I hear his shoulders pop from his own tension.

"Honestly? I don't know. I thought I wanted to just..." he waves a hand "...live my life at court." He trails off, looking down at his fingers. Rubbing the spaces between them as if he's used to more rings than the one small band he has on his right hand. "To be someone. You know?"

I sit back. *Valtair* wants to be someone? "But you are someone. I know who you are. Everyone knows who you are."

"But am I, though? Or am I just my father's son? The crown prince's friend? The court rake everyone whispers about, like they know me?"

"But you're here with me. That's something to me." I

know the wine is sloshing to my brain, and...other places...
but I still lean forward, and reach for his hand. "You're
someone to me."

He stills, his eyes on me. Leaning a little, his hand
clasped in mine.

We've moved closer without meaning to. Both leaning
toward each other now. His knee almost touching mine.

I should pull back.

But I don't.

"Tell me something true," he says. "Something you've
never told anyone. I'll go first. I've never kissed a man I
want to marry."

That statement...goes straight down, and my breath
catches at the sudden heat.

"I've been lying my whole life," I say.

About who I am. What I want. Even to myself, for
most of it. And now that I've stopped lying, now that I'm
trying to be honest, I don't know if I'm doing what I want
most in the world right.

I don't know if I'm being myself right.

But here is this gorgeous man, who is sitting knee to
knee with me.

Who isn't what the people say about him.

Who's running from his own demons, too.

"That's...also familiar," he says softly. His eyes locked
on mine.

There's a yearning there that I've never seen in anyone

before. He's watching me like I hold an answer to a question he didn't think he'd ever have answered.

And that...that might be the most dangerous thing of all. Because I can feel a tugging in my heart that isn't just heat now.

That sees an answer to a question I've asked in him, too.

Then he laughs softly. Almost nervously. Valtair, nervous?

"We're both a mess, aren't we? Gods. Why would anyone want a mess like me?"

He's breaking my heart by just spilling out his.

"Because you're good at making people feel safe," I say. Because he already knows he's beautiful—that's not why he thinks he's undesirable. Why someone made him think that—his father?

My anger spikes at that, too, and this time for him.

Surprise flickers across his face, and maybe pleasure.

"That's not who I am at court," he says, and brushes a hand through the air, as if he's writing words. "Lord Valtair: the one who makes us feel safe. Yeah, no. It doesn't work."

"Then the court doesn't know you."

The words hang between us.

Like the world, like everyone I know, doesn't know me.

His gaze settles on my mouth. Lingers there.

My pulse jumps.

And the air thickens. Every point of awareness narrows—the way he's looking at me, the slight parting of his lips, the rise and fall of his chest.

Ohhh this is dangerous.

I want him. I want him like I've never wanted anyone before.

And I've never wanted anyone as a man before. Not like this.

I've never had anyone look at me like this before. He's looking at me like a man. With desire.

And maybe I've never had anyone look at me like that as a woman, either.

The few times I ever messed around with a man, it was awkward, and painful. More for their benefit than mine.

I've had sex exactly twice and enjoyed it not at all.

I want to close the distance and find out if the taste of his wine is still lingering on his lips. If he'll taste the taste of mine.

I want those elegant hands on my skin. Want to be touched as myself, as Morgan, as the man I am and the man I'm becoming.

The man I want to live the rest of my life as.

But—

But, gods.

I can't have that.

I cannot have any good thing like this. Ever. Or it will all go away.

He won't be able to trust me. He won't want me anymore, because if he finds out my body doesn't match—

Fear surges like bitter iron in my mouth.

Valtair pulls back. "Morgan? What's wrong?"

Everything. Nothing.

I'm terrified. Exhilarated.

I want this more than I've wanted anything in my life, and I didn't know I wanted something like this so badly until the moment is here.

I want—I want more than a fumble in the dark. I want more than his body.

Downstairs—voices. Rising. My brother's voice? I keep listening for his voice to get louder, to come up the hall, to bang open this door, to demand to take me home.

And I keep telling myself that he still doesn't know I'm a man. He's just grasping at the wind, he's trying to cover every place I could be.

I tell myself Valtair's here, and he does offer some safety. Though I can also tell he's not a fighter. I could more likely protect him if it comes to it—I grew up training with my younger brother, because I was willing, and my younger brother needed someone to spar against. That, at least, my father allowed me.

Can I hope my brother's left already? But, he'll probably stay the night in this rain.

My whole body tenses.

Valtair's hand grips mine again. His thumb moves in small circles. "Breathe. You're safe with me."

And I know I am. I know that with the same intensity as the need rising again through my fear.

The voices downstairs fade. Become part of the background noise again.

Our knees are still touching. And holding his hand, the space between us is almost none.

"Come here," I say. And feel the husk of my voice, feel the audacity of asking him to come to me.

"I'm here."

"Closer."

He shifts closer and offers his other hand.

Take it, and everything changes.

Don't take it, and I'm still running. Still hiding. Still afraid.

I take his hand.

He pulls me up.

"Where do you want to go?" he asks.

He's not asking if I want to leave the room.

I reach up and trail a trembling hand along his cheekbone, edging down toward his jaw. Toward his lips.

His breath catches, his eyes intent on mine.

Valtair watches me as he cups my jaw. Gentle. Careful.

"Tell me to stop," he says.

My heart hammers so loud he must hear it. Must feel it in the air between us.

Maybe I should tell him to stop.

I should pull away.

Because he'll push me away the moment we start losing our clothes.

Is it too much to just want the sweetness of this moment? Is that a betrayal of him?

But I *am* a man. I am. It's not wrong for me to want this, or want it with him.

"I don't want you to stop," I whisper. "Do you...want me to..."

His eyes darken. Pupils blown wide in the candlelight.

He leans in.

Slowly.

Giving me time.

Giving me space to change my mind, damn him. How can anyone think he's anything but a gentleman?

I don't change my mind.

His breath ghosts across my lips. Wine and something uniquely him beneath that overpowering cologne.

I suddenly decide I like his cologne. It's fitting—like him, his outer mask to hide his softness beneath.

The distance between us narrows to nothing.

My eyes flutter closed.

And yes, his lips taste like wine.

CHAPTER 4

AWAKENING

MORGAN

When I first saw him in the court all those years ago, I was arrested, but I'd seen him as a man of the court, too. Someone who was a part of that vaunted world that my family brushed up against but never seemed to inhabit.

Impossibly out of reach.

I kiss him back, my body awakening with a need I've ignored for far too long. And I never, ever thought that need would be aimed at this man. Or that he'd need me back.

His hand slides from my jaw to the back of my neck, fingers threading into my short hair. I'm too enthralled to be embarrassed by my hair—it was the best I could do in the near dark before I slipped out of my family's manor house and away.

Valtair's touch sends heat down my spine. I've never been touched like this before. Never.

I tell the part of my mind screaming that this can't go further to shut the hell up.

Valtair makes a sound against my mouth and pulls me closer. We're standing now, though I don't remember rising. My hands find his chest, feeling the steady thrum of his heartbeat through the fine silk of his shirt.

He tastes like the southern valley wine, sweet and bitter all at once.

His other hand finds my waist, possessive.

The room tilts slightly—wine and want making everything soft around the edges.

I could stay here. In the heat of his mouth, the press of his body against mine, the way he touches me like I matter.

He's kissing me because he sees me as a man. And the triumph of that almost drives me sober.

His hand moves up my back, then slides around toward my chest—

My eyes spring open, and I jump back, stumbling into the chair, banging the back of my leg.

"Shit!"

Valtair lunges for me, only partially in time to catch my fall.

"What?" he gasps. "Did you hear—"

He looks toward the door. Then back to me.

And I see hurt flickering across his face. He licks his lips.

But I'm shaking my head, scrambling to get up, my heart hammering.

No, it's not him. He's perfect.

I can't catch my breath, the binding garment is too tight. I desperately want to take it off, or loosen it at least, but that—that would be far worse. And anyhow, impossible.

I scrub a hand across my face. It comes back wet. Am I crying?

Gods. I feel my face heating so hard, and I know I'm flushing crimson, and I *hate* that. I hate that I always flush when I'm upset, my body betraying me yet again.

"Morgan," Valtair says, and he shifts, and something else comes into his eyes now. "Are you hurt? I thought I felt—are you bandaged?"

I close my eyes. Relief hitting me along with the sense of everything I've wanted slipping away from me. Everything I know I can't have.

But I open my eyes again, and the look in Valtair's eyes —not like he wants to go punish whoever made this theoretical injury, but like he wants to comfort me now— catches my breath.

He's a man of the court.

I never expected him to be this kind, even if I saw glimpses of that in him before.

My body responds to that kindness with another surge of heat, blasting past the coolness of my fear.

And maybe I won't have another chance to know if I can be loved as I am. To know if another man will see me as I am.

I swallow. "I—I'm a man."

He blinks. "Yes...I can see that." Then his face falls. "Gods. How old are—"

"I'm twenty-three, no, that's not it."

He nervously shakes out his hands. "Okay, then, is this your first time? We don't have to—I'm sorry I assumed—"

I step closer, close my hands around his fluttering fingers. "You didn't assume anything."

And I shiver, and I know my courage is waning, so I shore it up. I shove it out. I have to.

"I wasn't born a man."

Valtair's eyes flick between mine, his brow furrowed. He looks down the length of me, then back up to my eyes. "But you're a man."

It's not a question.

"Yes."

He blinks again, takes a breath. "Then I don't see the problem."

I shudder, and he catches me, pulling me to him, pressing my face to his shoulder. Holding me while I struggle through exactly three sobs before I can pull myself together.

"Is that why your family is after you?" he asks quietly.

Gods. I don't want to tell him that. That feels like one detail pulled from the depth of my being too far.

But I nod into his shoulder. His grip on me tightens, and I pull back to see anger in his eyes again.

"They don't know," I say quickly. As if I need to defend them.

And he sighs out. Cups a warm hand to my cheek.

His gaze is heating again.

"I want to kiss you again. Can I?"

Not trusting myself to speak, I nod.

He leans in again, and this time, his touch is...the same.

I expected him to be more gentle, like I'm fragile. Or patronizing. Anything but the exact same heat.

I make a moan deep in my throat, and he pauses.

"Is this okay?"

"Yes. Gods. Please. Yes."

I seize his neck and pull him back to me roughly, and his hunger is right there with me.

We stumble backward. Bump against the chair again, then tumble towards the bed.

I sit, pulling him down with me. He follows, one knee on the mattress beside my hip, leaning over me until he can settle beside me, never breaking the kiss.

"Morgan," he murmurs against my mouth. "Tell me if I do something you don't like."

"Yeah," I say, entirely preoccupied with unbuttoning his shirt.

His own hands hesitate, then he begins to unbutton mine.

The binding garment I carefully made is tight against me, reeking more than I'd like of sweat and the road. And now I'm wishing I had some of his overpowering cologne, too.

The fabric is only a little lighter than my own skin tone, I dyed it carefully with herbs.

Valtair's fingers hover against it, but he doesn't try to undo the fastenings down the sides.

"Do you want me to—"

"No," I say.

So instead, he shifts to pull off his boots, then helps me out of mine.

He pauses with one of my boots in hand. "Huh. A local craftsman's work?"

I look down. I took one of the stable hand's clothes and boots, knowing he was most similar in size to my own lean but stocky frame. The boots—I know he'll miss them.

They're sturdy leather, with red-stained ravens winding around the heels. Syran was proud of those boots that he made.

I'll find a way to send them back.

"Um. Yeah."

The boots are no longer important as we both focus on divesting the rest of our clothes, me unbuttoning his shirt all the way down, him carefully undoing the laces on my pants, until we're down to our small clothes. And then he shimmies out of his.

Every inch of this man is so beautiful I could cry.

He reaches toward the last ties at my waist, then stops again, looking into my eyes.

Fear seizes me up again. Because I can see he wants me, oh that's so very clear.

And the rolled-up sock I'd stuffed into my underwear looks lumpy and...not like what it should be.

My cheeks burn again.

Will I watch his desire fade when he sees the whole of me?

I don't look at him as I carefully undo the ties and push my small clothes down, then off.

But his desire hasn't faded.

And neither has the hunger in his eyes.

"You're fucking beautiful," he says.

He trails a hand across my cheek, leans in to kiss my neck.

I shiver, and can't breathe again. I don't want to take the binding garment off, but—

I press a palm to his cheek. "Let me loosen it."

He nods and waits with rocking impatience as I fumble with the long row of clasps on one side.

Then his hands are darting in, helping me pop most of them.

"Leave the top," I say.

And gods, I hope I'm not cooling the mood.

But when his mouth takes mine again, the heat is right at the surface again. And I surrender to my need, and his.

I run my hands down his chest, down.

I need him. I need him to fill everywhere that's empty within me.

I need him like I've never needed anything, or anyone, before.

And when I cry out, when he shudders against me, when we collapse together in a tangle of limbs and racing hearts—

I know I'm not the same. I will forever not be the same.

Chapter 5

Warmth

Morgan

I wake to warmth beside me, and for a long moment, I just revel in it.

This is something I've dreamed of. The heat of someone I care about, who cares about me, warming me through the night.

For three heartbeats, I float. I don't try to remember where I am. I only know I'm pressed against bare skin, that there's an arm draped across my waist, fingers resting on my hip. That someone breathes slow and even against the back of my neck, prickling the hair.

Slowly, the warmth turns to panic.

Then memory floods back.

Valtair's room. The wine. My confession.

And his casual acceptance. Like nothing else was even an option.

His mouth on mine. His hands. His hands *all over* me.

And him inside me. *Gods.*

The way I've never been so full, so whole before.

The sound of my name in his voice when we—

I carefully maneuver one hand to touch my chest. My binding garment is still on, though loosened at the side and not really binding at the moment. Still, it's a barrier. I don't have to see what's beneath it, and so he didn't, either. I sigh out in relief.

But I'm still naked under these satin sheets, these wool blankets, and so is he. Our legs are tangled together. His chest rises and falls against my back, and I can feel every plane of muscle, every shift of breath.

He's not a heavily muscled man, but he's fit in his own way. Sure of himself and his body. Sure of his hands and what he does with them.

Oh what he does with them.

Heat floods my face again. Gods, had that all actually happened? But I'm here, still in his arms. And thank the gods of all the seasons I never stopped taking the herbs that ward away pregnancy.

Gods. No.

I should move. Get dressed. Sneak out before anyone sees.

Now, in the pre-dawn gray, I'm wondering what the hell I've done.

And what he'll think when the wine's fully worn off.

Drink might have made him mellow and a little maudlin, like it made me brazen.

Will he be so forgiving in the daylight?

I don't move.

Dawn light seeps through the shutters. The fire died hours ago, and the room is cold enough that frost etches patterns on the window glass. But here, cocooned in blankets with Valtair warm against me, even knowing I should go...I feel just a moment of safety.

I don't want that moment to end.

He's not yet awake. Nothing has changed. He's warm, and his words from last night, his *everything* from last night, warms every part of me.

His arm tightens around my waist. Not awake yet, just shifting in sleep, but the movement presses us closer together. I bite my lip against the want that's rising in me again. Gods, again?

What is wrong with me? I want to turn over and kiss him awake.

And what if I want to kiss him awake again and again?

Was it the wine that made me brazen, or...him?

Valtair makes a soft sound, and his face presses into the hollow where my neck meets my shoulder. His breath ghosts across my skin.

I close my eyes. Let myself have this for one more moment.

Then his lips brush my neck—not quite a kiss, just contact—and heat shoots straight through me.

"Morning," he murmurs against my skin. Sleep-rough and low. His hand slides from my hip to my stomach, palm flat and warm. "You awake?"

My heart hammers. "Yeah."

"Good." His mouth moves to the spot just below my ear. This time it's definitely a kiss. "I was hoping last night wasn't a dream."

I turn in his arms. It takes some maneuvering under the blankets, but then I'm facing him and the want in his eyes matches what's burning under my skin.

"Not a dream," I manage, and stare into his deep brown eyes, feeling my own challenge.

He can see the binding garment, loose though it is. He can lift the covers and see more.

Not that he didn't see everything last night.

But—but the wine haze is gone now. My temples ping with the start of a hangover.

Won't everything be different in the daylight?

But his smile is lazy, full of sleep and growing hungry again.

He reaches up to cup my jaw. "Good," he says again, and then he's kissing me on my lips.

It is different from last night. Less desperate, but somehow *more*. Like we have time. Like this could be the start of something instead of the end.

His hand slides into my short hair, and I press closer, greedy for the heat of him, the taste of him, the solid realness of his body against mine.

When we break apart for air, we're both gasping. My leg curled over his. Valtair's thumb traces my cheekbone.

I need him so much I'm going to explode.

"Let's just stay in bed," he says. "We'll order up breakfast. Or, uh, maybe just lunch. Do you have somewhere urgent to be? I can take a day more."

The words crack something open in my chest. I want to. I want to so badly it aches in the deepest part of me. I want to stay in this bed, in this moment, in the warm circle of his arms and pretend the rest of the world doesn't exist.

But it does.

"I need to—" I start, then stop. What? What do I need?

Use the chamber pot. That suddenly becomes my top concern.

I extract myself from the blankets, and the lack of Valtair's warmth hits me like a blow. The room is freezing. My skin prickles, and my breath mists in the air. I grab my shirt from where it's puddled on the floor and yank it on —it goes halfway to my knees—though it does little against the cold.

The chamber pot is in the corner near the window. I

take care of business quickly, trying not to think about how exposed I feel.

"I'm not watching," he calls, his voice still heavy with sleep.

And I vent a laugh because—because it's ridiculous, isn't it?

It is.

And yet he's still sensitive to my concern.

And I'm feeling more confident as I pull my shirt back down. The rest of my clothes are on the floor, I'll just retrieve—

I pass the window and stop breathing.

There in the inn yard, barely visible in the pre-dawn light, sits a carriage among several others, but I know this one. Black lacquered wood. Brass fittings that catch what little light there is. And on the door, picked out in gold leaf—

My family's crest.

Two ravens, wings spread. The symbols of my father's house.

My brother's still here.

I was hoping—gods, I was hoping that he would have moved on, though I knew with the rains that probably wasn't true.

And maybe I could stay here holed up with Valtair, but what if my brother asks more intently? What if he remembers that I did wear trousers, what if he puts it together that I might not be traveling as a woman?

"Morgan?" Valtair's voice cuts through the roaring in my ears. "What is it?"

I can't answer. Can't move. I'm staring at that carriage, at the crest that used to mean something like home but has come to mean a prison.

The bed creaks as Valtair rises, and I hear him rustling around until he finds his pants.

He stubs his toe on the bedpost and swears worse than the boatmen who come by the river near my family's estate.

That gets a small smile out of me.

Valtair buckles his pants as he hobbles over to me. "Fuck, it's cold."

But he stops behind me, craning around to see past me.

"My brother's carriage," I say.

"Which one?"

Should I tell him? My family is *barely* high nobility. A barony at the border.

"The black carriage. With the raven crest."

He shifts to look at it.

Then back to me.

He does recognize the crest. And then I watch as a different recognition blooms in his eyes.

I swallow and step back.

Because how can he keep seeing me as a man, when he saw me before, when he does remember, when my body—

He catches my hand.

"Morgan."

I flinch, and he pulls back.

But he says, "Talk to me."

"I have to go." The words scrape out of my throat. "Now."

"Morgan—"

I back into the room, gathering up my clothes, shoving them on.

"I won't go back."

"I won't let them take you—gods, you're your own man."

"That," I hiss, "is the problem." I stop buttoning my shirt long enough to look up at him. "They don't see me as anything but an extension of their own purposes. And maybe—maybe in the end they wouldn't even care if I am a man. But it messes up their marriage plans for me. And the inheritance. They already have several men lined up for me, and none of them would—"

None of those men would ever see me for who I am, I know. I know all of them. Maybe in the capital of Barella, in the palace, with men like Valtair, things are different. My uncles are married, that's never been an issue, though I know generations ago it once was.

But for me to deprive my family of the connections they wish to make because I'm actually a man?

And yes, then there's the problem of my younger brother's inheritance. Because if he suddenly has an older brother, and not a sister, that...could get ugly.

It's safer, so much safer, for me just to leave. To disappear. For them to forget about me.

"I have to go," I say again.

My trousers—where the fuck are my trousers? There, in a heap by the bedpost. I grab them, nearly fall trying to get my legs through while my hands shake so hard I can barely hold the fabric.

"Morgan—"

"I can't wait. If they find me here—if they find me with you—I can't involve you."

"I don't care about that. And we'll figure something out."

"There's nothing to figure out!" My voice cracks, and I can't look at him, though he's come close again. Hovering.

I'm dressed now except for my boots. I drop into the chair and grab them, but my hands are shaking too badly to work the laces.

Valtair crouches in front of me. Takes the boot from my hands. And I barely see him for the blur in my eyes.

I swipe at my eyes angrily.

"Morgan. Let me help you. Please."

"You're a lord of the kingdom," I snap back. "I'm not —you can't politically help a nobody, it would hurt your—"

He unlaces the boots and then pulls me up. Holds me steadily and helps me step into them.

"So are you," he says quietly.

But I shake my head. "No. I'm not—I'm not ever going back to that."

"Then stop fighting me and let me help you."

I sniff, long and hard.

Then bend to tie the laces on my boots. His hands resting on my hips, holding me steady.

He's quiet. Giving me space, maybe, or maybe thinking about how what I've said is true.

He's the son of the former Minister of Finance. He's the best friend of the man who will someday be the king.

I'm a runaway baron's son who can no longer claim that inheritance in any way.

Finally, he asks, "Where will you go?"

"I don't know. Away. Somewhere they won't look."

"That's not a plan."

"It's the only plan I have."

I finish tying my boot laces then straighten, looking up into his eyes.

The look on his face nearly slays me.

He doesn't want me to go.

I don't want to go away from him either.

But I have to.

Can't he see that? He has to see that. He's a man of the court, he sees people every day, I know he can read the inevitability of this ending.

This was a moment, this night together. I will cherish it forever. But it was just a moment.

I knew it couldn't last.

"I'm sorry," I say. "I—thank you. For everything. But I have to—"

"I know." His hands tighten on my knees. "I know you have to go. So I'm going with you."

Chapter 6

Leaving

Valtair

"I know you have to go. So I'm going with you."

The words leave my mouth before I've thought them through.

But I mean them. I would—I will—say them again.

Morgan stares at me. His eyes are wide, from fear and something else—the ghost of what we shared last night still lingering between us.

Gods, last night. When was the last time I felt something that *real* with someone?

Years ago, maybe.

But...maybe I've never felt anything this real before.

He was terrified that I'd reject him, I know that.

And no, men who weren't raised as men and women who weren't raised as women aren't as common or always as accepted, but I was with a man like him before, years ago. This wasn't my first time.

But I think it was his, as himself. He trusted me with that.

He gave all of himself to me last night. And I'm achingly aware of what a gift that was.

He held me so tenderly I felt I might shatter from the gentleness of it. I'm used to being the one my partners expect to be sure of myself.

I'm not used to being cared for. Like Morgan was gentling my own hurts and fears, too.

Because he actually saw them. And doesn't think my position or my family negates the ache of them.

It terrifies me how much I want his touch again. How much I want to give him in return.

"Valtair, this isn't your problem." Morgan's voice cuts through my thoughts. Low, urgent.

He pulls away from me and backs toward the door, and I hate that he thinks I might stop him. That I'm another person trying to control where he goes, who he is.

And gods, how did I end up here again, trying to throw myself between someone and whatever problems they're facing? Most of the time, people don't appreciate it. Or try to take advantage. That's the court, and they're always—*always*—aware of my social position. Who my father is and who my friends are.

But that's not Morgan, I know that's not him.

And maybe this time it's not just that Morgan needs help.

He made me feel like someone worth more than the shallow flings and social games of the court.

He *saw* me, my drunken, maudlin, far too deep in my own truths and up my own ass self.

And he opened himself to me, and didn't look away. He wrapped himself around me, and cradled my head in his hands as I came. As he did, too.

I've never been held like that before.

He was terrified that I'd reject him, and yet he held *me.*

"Well, it's my problem now," I say.

"Valtair, I'm sorry—"

"No, I mean, I want it to be." I know that's not the right way to say it, but I'm still trying to shake off sleep. I reach for my shirt. "I'm not letting you step into that mess alone. I'm coming with you."

He's standing near the door, but not moving yet to open it. Watching me warily.

"You don't know my brother. Or my father."

"Well, they don't know me. And I do know your father's reputation. A little. That one Harvest Festival, um, your father was asking mine for more taxes to be funneled to your district. I know that meeting didn't end well. My father wasn't happy about it. So."

Morgan makes a face that's somewhere between annoyance and exasperation.

He runs a hand through his bed-messed hair, making it stand on end.

And my attention arrests there, because he's absolutely adorable.

I want to kiss him again.

Run my hands through that badly cut hair again. I think I like that cut, I should convince him to keep it. Cut it badly again.

Morgan's eyes lock on mine again, and his lips part. He still hasn't moved.

One half of his mouth slowly tips up in a smirk, and that does…interesting things to my insides.

But he shakes his head. "Okay. Then, you know I still have to go, and that makes it even more vital you don't get involved, if your father and my father have history—what would your father think if—"

"I don't give a particular fart what my father thinks this morning," I say, and yank my shirt on. The fabric is cold, and underneath it my skin prickles with the memory of the heat of Morgan pressed against me. The taste of him. The sound he made when I—

Gods, I have to cool myself down or I won't be able to think, and I need all my wits right now.

So I think of the last man I slept with at court, two months ago now, a rich merchant's son who was exquisitely experienced. I felt pleasure, yes.

But little more.

That cools me more than I'd like to admit just now.

The court likes to think I sleep with a different man every night. I haven't exactly done anything to sway them from that notion. It's a convenient social shield. But I'm pickier than they think. Most of the time.

And I know which man I want now.

I look back up at Morgan, and he's watching me.

What would it be like to sleep with the same man every night?

My skin crawls as I hear my father again shouting that I need to settle down, to think about the family reputation, for once.

And the thought of sleeping with one person recoils in me even as I try to push past that directive from my father to reach for something I actually do want.

As if I don't think about the family reputation every day. As if that wasn't drilled into me since childhood.

I can be who I am and also uphold the family reputation, can't I?

I button my shirt with quick movements, keeping my eyes on Morgan even as he hovers by the door, looking more and more like he might bolt. Like he has to go, or he'll never go.

Then a cloud passes across his eyes. Morgan's gaze turns wary again, and he shifts his weight. "Are you helping because I was...born a woman?"

I jerk upright. "Gods, no. I wouldn't be that petty."

"Then why?" He balls his hands into fists. "Why are you helping me? You're a courtier—gods, you're the king's best friend—"

"Is that why you wanted to sleep with me?" I snap back, and regret it the moment it's out.

His eyes flash, and he takes a step back toward the door.

"Morgan, I'm sorry. It's—" I press a hand to my forehead. I'm hungover, and struggling to shake the lassitude of sleep, and our night together. My limbs all still feel warm and wobbly. "I'm sorry. It's why people usually want to sleep with me. Not you. I know not you."

He swallows. "Not me," he agrees.

I fish in my jacket pocket for the clasp I'd used on my hair yesterday and fumble behind me to pull it back. There isn't a good mirror in this room.

Morgan hesitates a moment, then comes behind me and holds my hair while I pull the clasp tight.

"Sorry," he says. Though I don't know exactly what he's apologizing for now.

I grip his wrist. "Let's just get you out of here, past your brother, then we can talk?"

He's still for a long moment, but finally, he nods.

I straighten and smooth down my coat. I probably should have changed. Gods, probably should have washed up, but, no time for that now.

I grab my travel bag—he doesn't have one—and head for the door.

But as I'm reaching for it, a door slams down the hall. Voices rise—louder now, heavy footsteps moving past. Someone shouts for the innkeeper.

Morgan goes pale.

And that would have to be his brother.

We wait, listening. The footsteps retreat, rattling down the stairs. The inn's common room isn't as noisy as it was last night, but more voices rumble up from below.

"Now," Morgan hisses. "I saw there's a servant's stairs at the back."

I sling my bag over my shoulder and follow him to the door. He cracks it open, peers into the dim hallway. Most of the doors are shut, the hallway itself quiet. But below us, the inn is stirring. Footsteps. The scrape of furniture. Clank of a spoon in a pot.

Morgan slips out, and I follow, keeping my footfalls light. The floorboards creak anyway, and I wince.

But no doors open, at least. No one calls out.

Morgan leads me to the back stairs—narrow and steep, the servants' route. He moves like he's done this before. Like trying not to be seen is muscle memory.

I follow, watching the tension radiate through his shoulders and back. He expects to be caught. To hear his brother's voice calling his name.

I'm tensed, too, for what I might have to do if his brother finds us. I'm not letting someone Morgan fears that much take him anywhere.

But that moment doesn't come.

We reach the ground floor in a crowded storeroom. The back door sits ahead, half-hidden behind stacked crates. Morgan makes for it without hesitation, his hand already on the latch.

I stay close behind him.

I'm not a fighter. I begged out of most weapons training when we were younger, and Torovan, being the friend that he is, argued my case. I was better at books, he said. And I was.

Books aren't going to help me here, though.

The door swings open.

Cold air stings my face, sharp with the smell of horses and wet earth. Morgan pauses in the doorway, silhouetted against the gray morning. He looks back at me.

There's fear in his eyes, but there's something else too. Something that might be hope.

Because yes, I'm still here. And he's still not alone in this. I won't let him be alone in this.

He steps out, and again, I follow.

When I woke with him warm in my arms this morning, I thought, *This. I want this.*

He can tell me he doesn't want me, and I will go away.

But I'm not letting anyone else tell me that.

And maybe I'm not a fighter when it comes to swords and daggers, but with him?

I'm not letting him go without the fight of my life.

CHAPTER 7

TRUST ME

MORGAN

"Do you have a carriage?" I ask in a low voice as we creep out into the fog-draped yard of the inn.

"I rented," Valtair says, "it's passed on. I was expecting to rent again today. Do you have a horse?"

I shift my shoulders in my coat. "No."

The fog is just clear enough that I can see his incredulous look. "Isn't your family from near the border? You *walked* all that way? What, did you *run* all that way if your brother is only catching up—"

I grip his arm and hiss, "Keep your voice down!"

I tense, looking around the inn wall toward the front entrance.

But no one else has come out, and the few people in

the inn yard seem to only be paying attention to their own mounts. The fog at least is muffling sounds.

Slowly, I let out a breath. Valtair twitches, and I ease my grip on his arm.

"I had to leave my horse in the last town back," I whisper. "She was exhausted, and I couldn't wait for her to rest. So I found a family that looked like they could use her and tied her to their barn."

I catch Valtair's eyes again, and find his gaze scorching. Angry, but not, I think, at me.

The horse wasn't one that I loved—I left my own beloved mare back at my family's home, knowing she'd be better cared for. Knowing I might have to ride hard and fast.

Knowing I might be pursued.

And that she could easily be identified as mine.

But still, the horse I left was one of my last connections to the life I had. And I'm sorry I drove her that hard. Sorry I couldn't stay while she recovered.

"Then, we'll find someplace you can stay out of sight, and I'll rent another carriage."

"I can't follow the road. I was going to go across the fields again, to the next town. I know there's another town to the east. My brother—"

"So we're just going to walk?" he asks. "I'm not exactly in practice."

"You don't have to come with me."

He gives me another look. "I'm coming."

"Well, just see me to the next town, then. Then you can resume your own journey."

Though the thought of leaving him behind makes my skin want to crawl.

But the risk of my brother trying to flag down carriages on the road, to ask for information or try to check if I'm among them, is too high.

A horse whinnies in the inn's stable nearby, and I jump.

"Come on," Valtair says. "We need to get properly out of here."

He readjusts his bag's strap over his shoulder, then sets off toward the town. It's out in the open, but I remind myself that I'm dressed as a man. That my brother, at least in this fog, wouldn't be able to know me on sight from a distance.

In the town, the streets are only just starting to come to life, the mist thick and cold enough that it hurts to breathe. Dawn light barely touches the rooftops, leaving the cobblestones in gray shadow. Cold seeps through my stolen boots, a little too large and clumsy on my feet.

I need to ditch these boots as soon as I can and find shoes that I can run in.

I'll find a way to send these boots back to the stable hand. I know he misses them.

Valtair walks close beside me. Close enough that I can hear his breathing, feel his presence as warmth beside me.

And though I know we've moved past it out of necessity, our argument from the inn still sits sourly between us.

I know last night meant something to him, too. I see it in the way he's reacting to me.

In the way he wants to protect me.

I flung at him that he still saw me as a woman—but I don't think he does.

He wants to protect me as a man.

And that terrifies me, too.

But gods, right now I'm glad he's here. It is good to not be alone.

I pull my scarf higher on my face. And I'm glad I decided to stash that in my bag when I had to ditch my other clothes with the loss of my horse. I couldn't carry a heavy bag on the road for days, just the small shoulder bag I have now that has a canteen, some dried meat, and bread. And the scarf, when I'm not wearing it.

I burn with embarrassment that Valtair knows this is all I have left in the world.

But I don't think I have his pity either. If all he'd shown me was pity, I would have found a way to slip away. I would have told him that no, he couldn't come.

I hadn't exactly expected to end up walking, without a horse or coins or even a plan other than to *go*.

But when I think about my brother, and my father, and my mother—when I think about going back, I tighten the scarf and trudge on.

It covers my nose and mouth, at least, and I'm doing my best to widen my gait, to walk as a man who'd been raised as a man.

The town gate is ahead. Just a few more streets.

I glance aside at Valtair, half convinced that he'll only see me to the gate and then make some excuse to go back to the warmth and comfort of the inn.

And should I have accepted his offer of a carriage? It's a greater risk, yes, but it could have taken me further, too.

But I just need to disappear. I *just* need to blend in, wherever I'm going, and then maybe stay for a while. Find some light work, in a stable, maybe, I'm good enough with horses. Or maybe finding a shopkeeper who needs help. Something.

Anything.

"You there! Boy!"

I jump, and every muscle locks.

The voice is coming from behind us. It's not my brother's, at least, but I don't dare to look back at who it is.

I tuck my chin down and let my messy hair fall forward. And I force myself to keep walking—running draws attention. Running means guilt.

Valtair subtly moves closer, giving me the barest look askance.

"I said stop!" Footsteps behind us, rapid on the wet stone.

Valtair's hand finds my elbow. His fingers squeeze once—a question.

"Don't stop," I breathe, barely audible.

But the footsteps are faster. A hand seizes my shoulder, spins me around. I duck my head further, keep my hair in my eyes, my face turned away from the weak dawn light.

But I see the man's pants, his coat. He wears my father's colors, and I finally place his voice. He's not a regular on our estate but someone my father occasionally hires to help when more help is needed.

He's broad-shouldered, weathered, a country tough. One of the retainers who rode in with my brother last night.

His eyes track down my body. Stop at my feet.

"Those boots." His voice goes hard. "Those are Syran's boots. Where'd you steal them?"

I swallow around a rock in my throat.

The boots. Gods, the *boots*. Syran the stable hand made them himself, I can't argue that there are others like them. They're one of a kind. The boots were a *mistake*.

"Bought them off a stable hand," I say. I keep my voice

level and deepened as far as I dare. The cold gives it a breathy rasp.

"Syran would never sell them! He was yelling about them going missing when we were leaving." The man steps closer. His breath clouds in the cold air between us, sour with last night's wine. "Look at me, you thief. I'm taking you to the constable!"

Valtair, still beside me, says, "I think there's been some mistake—"

The man reaches for me again, but I dance back, years of drill practice with my father and brother kicking in.

My hands hang loose at my sides. Steady, despite the fear singing through my veins. My father taught me to fight alongside my brother—an indulgence, a game for him. Teaching his daughter the same skills as his son, because why not? She'd never need them.

He was wrong about that. About so many things.

I look up. Not at the man's face, but at his chest, his shoulder. Anywhere but his eyes.

"I said look at me, boy!"

"Hey," Valtair says, more firmly, "back off—"

My eyes meet the retainer's.

His brow furrows. His mouth opens—

I drive my fist into his jaw.

His head snaps to the side, and he staggers, more surprised than hurt I think, and I press forward. A blow to the stomach, the way my father showed me. Hard and fast. The man doubles over, gasping.

"Morg—" Valtair's voice cracks with alarm, and I glare at him before he can say my name.

Not that anyone in my family knows it. But I don't want my name on any of their lips.

The retainer recovers too quickly. He's been trained for real violence, not practice bouts in a nobleman's yard. His hand goes to his belt, comes up with a dagger.

"You little shit." He bares his teeth. "I'll take your fucking hand for this."

He lunges.

I twist aside but not fast enough—the blade whistles past my ribs, so close I feel the air move. My own knife is in my hand now, small and sharp and far too ornamental.

"Stop!" Valtair tries to move between us, and he's stupidly brave for that. But he has no weapons. And, I don't think, the training to use them even if he had.

"Valtair, back!" I yell.

The man's blade flashes.

Valtair jerks back, but the dagger catches him anyway, slicing through his coat.

He makes a sound—surprise, not yet pain—and stumbles backward, falling onto the ground.

Blood blooms dark against the fabric of his coat.

Everything narrows to a single point: Valtair's blood

on the cobblestones, his hand pressed to his side, his face going rigid as he holds up fingers wet with blood.

No.

No.

I told him this was my problem, not his.

He can't die. He *can't* die.

He's—he's who he is, he's someone who saw me.

He held me.

He's the only person in this world who's ever seen me as myself. All of me.

I cannot lose him.

I don't think. I move.

My hand closes on the retainer's wrist, twisting until I feel something grind. His dagger clatters away. I drive my knee into his groin, using his momentum to shove him backward into the wall.

Then I shove the heel of my hand at his nose and feel a solid crunch.

He yells and tries to swing at me. I duck, but he lands a blow on my cheek.

Pain explodes across my face, and I stagger a step back.

He grins through the blood running into his mouth.

It's the grin that makes me snap.

I know how to end this fight. I'm quick, and he's stronger, but slower. So I dart in beneath his next swing, grab his head with both hands, and slam it into the stone wall behind him.

Once.

His eyes roll back, and he drops.

Then there's silence, except for the ragged sound of breathing.

Which I realize is my own.

Nausea rolls over me.

Gods. Is he even still alive?

What did I just do?

But I turn. Valtair has both hands pressed to his side now, blood flowing far too freely between his fingers. His eyes are wide, fixed on me.

I can't worry about the man who tried to kill us.

I'm already moving to Valtair, kneeling down, my hands reaching for the wound before I'm even there.

"Morgan," he says shakily, "your face—"

"Let me see." I pull his hands away, lift the torn fabric of his shirt beneath his coat.

The cut runs along his ribs—not deep enough to hit anything vital, I hope, but long and bleeding steadily. And shit, I just pulled his hands away.

I press both my hands to it, applying pressure.

"Is it bad?" Valtair asks, voice tight.

"You're conscious," I say, trying to bring up every lesson I'd ever heard the weapons master giving my brother. "You're talking, that's good. But we need to get you somewhere I can clean and stitch this."

My hands are shaking.

"We need to move," he says, looking at the unconscious—or worse—retainer.

"I have to—"

Footsteps. Multiple sets, coming fast. Voices calling out in the mist.

We both freeze.

"—heard a shout—"

"—this way—"

My brother's voice, carrying through the fog: "Find them! Now!"

There's no time for us to move, and I don't know if Valtair can stand anyway. The street ahead is exposed. Behind us, my brother and his other man are approaching.

"Hold your wound," I say quickly. "Try not to look as injured as you are. I'm your servant, okay?"

"What are you—"

"Do you trust me?"

He stares at me for a heartbeat. He shifts his own hands back to press on the wound, then nods.

And lets me pull him to his feet, only stumbling a little before he leans against me.

My overriding, paralyzing thought is we can't have my brother insisting on calling for a healer, elemental or not. Because even if he doesn't recognize me, if a healer tries to examine me, too—

I round my shoulders, keep my eyes on the cobblestones, and try to prop up the wavering Valtair.

I'm a servant here.

I'm nobody.

I do have practice—I snuck out of my house the last few months in men's clothing stolen from servants. And it worked mostly.

Until my mother recognized me a few days ago and yelled that I was going to ruin the family's reputation by masquerading as the staff, and what would my future husband think of me?

I try to pull my scarf higher, but there's blood on my fingers, and I know I'm just smearing my face. But maybe that's a good thing, too.

But I know my brother. He's not kind, but he is relentless in his pursuit of what he thinks is right. And what he thinks is right just now will be dependent on the next few moments.

My brother rounds the corner of a stone house with two more men, one recruited from the inn, maybe.

He stops when he sees us.

Then takes in the scene: his unconscious retainer sprawled on the damp stone, blood still running from his injured nose—and maybe he isn't dead.

But then my brother looks up at Valtair and me, two strangers standing over his injured man.

His lip curls in a snarl.

What hits me, in that moment, isn't fear.

It's how much we do actually look alike, and more so

now with my hair hacked shorter, dressed in men's clothes.

My brother is living the life I will never have.

And my throat closes around a burn so tight I can't, for a moment, breathe.

I keep my head down. I'm just a servant, with his employer, caught in a street fight. That's it.

When I speak, my tight throat helps coarsen my voice. I try to use the accent of the marshes two days' ride from my family's estate, nothing like my own. My maid growing up was from those marshes.

"My lord was attacked." I gesture to Valtair with my chin and wipe my face again to smear more blood. "This bastard and another tried to rob us. The other one ran away."

It feels like I'm watching someone else speak with my mouth. Like I've split in two—part of me screaming inside while something else moves my body and shapes my words.

But it's not like all the times lately where I've had to split myself in two, to pretend to be a woman when I know I'm not. All those times, which got more and more excruciating in the last weeks until I couldn't—*could not*—take it anymore.

My brother's eyes fix on me.

But I don't meet his gaze. I don't look up. I can pretend like this, I can be someone else.

Just don't, ever, make me be *her* again.

My brother's attention shifts to Valtair. "Who are you?"

Valtair leans more heavily on me, trying to straighten despite the blood soaking his shirt. He lifts his chin. Every inch the offended nobleman.

"Lord Valtair, son of Count Valtair, of the royal palace." His voice could freeze water. "And you are?"

My brother's whole manner changes. The wariness is still there, yes, but now I see calculation beneath it. He's talking to someone whose family has power.

He does, at least, recognize Valtair's name, if not exactly remembering his face. He was younger than me when we were last at the palace in Barella.

"Lord Valtair." He gestures to the unconscious retainer. "That's one of my men. Did you do this?"

"My manservant defended me," Valtair says, and his voice sounds almost normal. Like he's not currently trying to keep his blood inside his body. "And I will reward him handsomely for doing so. Do see that your men don't try to rob passers-by in the future, yeah?"

I watch my brother out of the corner of my eye.

I watch his fists flex. But after a moment, he nods.

"Yes, my lord. Of course. My most sincere apologies. Are you—you are hurt, sir? Can I send for a healer—I don't even know if there's a healer in this town—"

My brother is starting to sound panicked. And I don't want to linger.

"No," Valtair says, and I hear the pain in his voice now. We need to end this, and quickly. "My man will see to me. He is an elemental healer. Good day, sir."

I stiffen, my ears ringing. Because—because how can Valtair know that?

It was the very last thing that tipped my decision to run.

And they say that elementalists sometimes manifest magic that otherwise would remain latent during moments of deep stress.

A few days ago, I screamed silently into my hands and froze the wine in the glass beside me.

Valtair swivels us both away, and we start to hobble away from my brother.

My neck prickles, waiting to see if my brother will protest, but he doesn't.

He never recognized me. Not that I wanted him to, but—

But maybe I also did. Maybe I wanted to be seen by someone I know. Someone I do, in my heart, care about.

Even if I loathe him, too.

"Well, he's alive," I hear my brother say as I stumble away with Valtair, and the tightness in my chest eases a little. Gods. I didn't kill my brother's man. I don't have that on my conscience, at least.

"Get him up," I hear my brother say. "Back to the inn."

My brother will hear a different story when the retainer wakes, and my stomach twists. That moment before I hit him, the man almost looked like there was a spark of recognition.

Or maybe not. I can't know.

Maybe it would be better if he had died. Even if the whole of me revolts at that thought.

Then their footsteps retreat, and our footsteps are the only ones I hear.

CHAPTER 8

WATER

Morgan

Valtair's breaths are getting more ragged.

"I need," he gasps, "to sit. I can—" He shudders. "I just need to sit."

Does he know I'm an elementalist? I'm a water elementalist, yes, but not yet trained in anything. I can't heal him. I can barely even feel the sense of water unless I concentrate. And I've been trying very hard not to since that first day with freezing the glass.

"Maybe there is a healer in this town," I venture. "I could try to find—"

"I don't need—I can take care of it. I just need to sit, and need time. And probably more food, because it burns away my energy to work on myself. Much more. Than others. Ahh—"

He staggers, and I sweep my gaze around the street

we're on, spotting a small open lean-to with piled up hay. It's not really cover, but it's better than the open, and it's close by. I steer him towards it.

Somewhere down the street a door bangs open, and a woman steps out, bellowing to a child behind her.

I hear the creak and slap of opening shutters nearby, the snapping shake of a rug.

The town is coming awake. And the light is brighter now, the fog starting to clear.

But there's no time to get through the gates and out of the town. I push Valtair down to sit in the hay.

"He didn't recognize you," Valtair gasps. He looks down at his wound and makes a queasy sound. "Your own brother. That is a shitty brother. I take it back, I regret every time I ever said I wanted siblings."

Is he babbling, or is he trying to distract himself? Is he going into shock?

"Yeah," I say. "My brother is shitty."

And maybe it's better this way. Maybe being invisible means being free.

But gods, it still hurts. It does.

I look around me for something to use as bandages, and finding nothing, turn to tug out my shirt and see if it's clean enough to tear.

"Don't," Valtair says, panting.

"But you need—"

"No, I need you to just wait and not spoil your

clothes, which," he gasps, "I think are your only clothes? I can handle this."

"You're still bleeding—" And I'm still going to tear my shirt.

He lets go of his wound long enough to knock my hand away.

"Just—will you wait? Okay? And...shield me from view."

"Valtair—"

"I'm—I'm an elementalist. Healer. Sort of." He glares up at me. "You don't tell anyone that, okay?"

I wet my lips, electricity running all the way down my spine and back up again.

He doesn't think I'm an elementalist, because *he is.*

And I know what it cost him to admit that. High nobility don't have elementalists in their families. Their blood is supposed to be above that.

Being an elementalist would instantly bring the family shame.

I take a breath.

"Uh...me too."

He looks up sharply in open shock. "You *what*? You're a water elementalist? You're a healer?"

"Not—I don't know—I mean, I only just found that out. A few days ago." I close my hand, feeling my magic humming in my palm as I think about it.

Gods, I'm thinking about it.

I open my hand again.

"Well—well, it'll be much harder, and take much longer, for me to try to heal myself," he says. And he's blinking hard, I can tell he's wavering. "Can I talk you through it? Do you know—know any of it—"

He gasps and holds both shaking hands back to his side. And maybe the cut was deeper than I'd thought. Maybe it's worse than I thought, maybe it did hit something vital inside, maybe infection is already setting in—I don't know enough about these things, only what I was taught to mend minor cuts and burns from training practice—

I look around at the street, we aren't exactly out of the way.

But at least I don't look like a noble right now.

Valtair even said that I was an elemental healer.

Gods, the *irony* of that truth. The irony that it was him.

And I'm not noble anymore, so what is the shame in this now?

"Okay," I say. "But I don't know if I can. I only—I've figured out how to freeze water, and I tried to stir water in a glass, and that sort of worked, and I did make my nails grow enough that I had to cut them." I wet my lips. I don't tell him that I tried, for hours, to make my face grow a beard.

Valtair's eyes track down my face, and his mouth

quirks despite the pain. "You grew your nails? Well, that's something, I guess. I started with erasing old training scars." He looks down, as if he can see them through his clothes. Then coughs and hisses at the pain.

"Okay," he wheezes, "hands on the wound. Feel for the water in my body."

"The water?"

"You know the feeling. People are mostly water." His voice is tight. "So feel that in me. Feel the currents of my body."

I crouch beside him. My hands hover over the torn fabric of his shirt as blood oozes through.

This is nothing like stirring water in a glass.

"I don't know if I can—"

"You can." His hand covers mine, guides it down to press against his side. I hiss at his soaked shirt, warm and sticky. Should I try to lift his shirt up completely? But he doesn't seem to think that's important. "Breathe," he says. "Reach for it."

I close my eyes. Try to find that hum I've felt before, something else I've marked in myself as forbidden.

That hum had been buzzing in my hands that day I froze the glass. That was the day I realized I was different in another way I didn't want.

I concentrate, like I concentrated in trying to make hair grow on my face.

Nothing happened then except my palms grew hot and I got a headache.

And...nothing happens now.

"Morgan." Valtair's voice is softer now. "Stop trying so hard."

My breath shudders out. I try, I really try—

Then take another breath and try not to try. Just to let it all go.

Because fuck it.

What does it matter anymore?

I am who I am, and trying to pretend otherwise will only bring me pain.

I'm a man, and I'm an elementalist.

And the distant humming in my palms grows stronger.

It's like opening my eyes underwater. I can almost see a current moving beneath my palms, cool and responsive.

"Got it? Good," Valtair gasps. "Now find where the flow is disturbed."

I strain again, reaching for something I don't think there are actually words for.

And I don't understand.

Until I do. The water in his body—blood and fluid and tissue—has a rhythm. A pattern. Where the blade cut him, the pattern breaks.

Okay. I can handle patterns. Like the necessary steps in a training sequence.

"I feel it."

"Shape it gently. Like smoothing out ripples in a pond."

I don't tell him that you can't smooth out ripples in a pond, not really. Has he spent any time at all in the country?

But I get his meaning. My magic rises, and it's terrifying how simple it is. How natural. The water responds, reorganizing, pulling tissue together, convincing flesh to remember how it should be.

Valtair makes a sound low in his throat.

"Gods," he gasps. "I can feel you."

I feel him too. Not the injury, but *him*. The shape of his fear, worn smooth by years of carrying it. The edges of his strength, honed sharp by necessity. The way he's held himself together through hiding beneath his court masks.

My hands grow warm against his skin. Magic flows between us like a current I can't dam. The wound is closing, the skin knitting.

"You're doing it," Valtair says, almost in disbelief. "If you haven't done this before—"

"I haven't."

"I didn't think it actually would—ow—*OW*!"

I jerk back, and Valtair presses his own hands to the wound again. He grimaces, and his eyes close. I'm not touching him, but, attuned as I am, I can almost feel his own magic working again at his wound.

"Did I do something wrong—"

"Just—give me a moment—"

My hands hover over him, but after a moment, he sighs out.

"I'm sorry," I say.

"Well, you got me far enough that I could get the rest."

He opens his eyes, and looks down at a puckering, angry scar. "That—will need some work later on."

"I'm sorry, Valtair—"

He closes one hand over mine. "You saved my life."

I stare back at him, and don't say anything. Because it's clogging in my throat that I'm the one who endangered his life to begin with. I didn't save anything.

Valtair holds up his other hand and, looking exhausted, and not looking at the street, and not looking like he cares if anyone sees, he lets water from the air, the receding mist around us, pool in his palm.

"You're water," he says. "Like me."

The morning sun is getting brighter, the water crystalline in his hand, until it starts to mix with the blood.

I don't know why my eyes sting, but they do. And his are shining, too.

He fills his palm with more water, then carefully washes the blood off his hands. It's still on his coat and his shirt, but he pulls his bag over and rummages for a moment, then comes out with a new shirt and coat.

I stand, shielding him from the view of any gawkers as he changes his shirt and coat. I don't know why, but letting him be seen right now, while he's still vulnerable, feels obscene.

Seen by anyone other than me.

"Is this why you ran, too?" he asks softly, buttoning up his coat.

He's far too perceptive. Seeing what I don't want anyone to see.

Well, but if someone has to see it, maybe it's good that it's him.

"Yes."

My throat can't get out more.

I just look at him. Then look away. Look down at my own hands and wonder if I can pull water from the air like he can to wash the blood off, too.

His blood is on my fingers, dark and drying. The evidence of what we've done. What we are.

What both of us are.

"You told me last night who you are," he says. "So… now you know me, too." He tries to shrug like it's less than it is.

We've moved past attraction. Past confession.

And what is there between us now?

Can water mix with lightning? Because that's what I'm feeling between us now, raw and untamed and ready to tear apart the sky.

I take a sharp breath and step back.

"We should go," I say.

Gods, my brother is still in the town.

And the morning fog is clearing. There's no cover, no shelter anymore.

Not that there truly had been.

I take another step away. "I should go."

Will he try to come with me again? Has he learned his lesson that staying near me is dangerous?

Another step back.

He follows.

CHAPTER 9

FRAGILE

VALTAIR/MORGAN

VALTAIR

Morgan keeps walking, and I follow.

I'm feeling exhausted even though it's morning, drained from the adrenaline, drained from my part in my healing. Drained from fear, just...gods.

I carefully heft my bag over my shoulder, lighter now less one expensive tailored coat and shirt, and follow Morgan. And he doesn't tell me not to.

His steps are loud and sure, just short of urgent. But I almost can't breathe with the panic I know he's feeling.

I just met him. Nevermind all those years ago—that wasn't actually him, not who he really is. And we never talked then, anyhow.

I shouldn't care this much for someone I only spent one night with.

But then, I was well on the path to caring even before we spent the night together, I know that. I know that with a clarity that sits in my stomach like iron.

I would follow this man anywhere, if he lets me.

We reach the town gate and pass through it—it's not guarded. This is a rural town along a well-traveled road, but not a city that needs guarded.

Outside the gates, the road lies muddy from yesterday's rain, the sky still gray but the sun peeking out too brightly.

My breath mists in the cold air as I walk. So does his.

Does he even know where he's going other than "away?"

I can still feel where his hands pressed against my side. The warmth of his magic flowing through me.

He doesn't think it was such a big thing what he did, learning that quickly. I was desperate to even try to teach him something like that—and yes, he hadn't finished it completely, wouldn't have finished it well, but he got that far.

He has magic like mine.

He knows the pain of a family that tries to push you in directions you don't want to go.

Would he...would he be someone my father would accept?

But gods, how can I think that. How can I lay that on him? How can I expect anything of him at all, when all of him right now is being stripped away?

And now he's walking away from me, faster, like he hopes to outrun me.

"Morgan." I jog to catch up, grimacing at the still-healing wound in my side, and reach for his arm.

He flinches from my touch. Actually flinches.

My hand drops. "Wait."

"I can't." He doesn't slow. His shoulders are hunched inward, making himself smaller. "My brother's still in town. I need to be gone before—actually, I do need to go off the road—" He turns straight into a copse of bushes.

And I'm almost certain now he's crying too hard to see.

"I said I'll come with you," I say, pushing after him through the heavy brush. He half runs up a short incline, reaches a cluster of trees, and stops, panting, against one of the trunks. Then slips around the other side of it, out of sight.

My heart gallops, and I rush to climb up the slope, too, to have him back in sight.

But he's right there, still on the other side of the tree. I almost collide with him and manage to put my hand out just in time to stop myself on the trunk.

And then we're too close. I catch his scent, musky and slightly sour from travel or maybe last night or maybe fear, and I don't *care*, I want to devour him. I want to pull him against me. I want to not let him run into whatever danger he's running into, and shield him from the danger behind him.

And I've never, ever felt that way about anyone before. Not like this.

He stares up at me, his dark eyes wide. His cheeks streaked with tears.

"Don't," he says.

"Come with me to the palace. To the capital. I can find you a position at court. You can start over—"

He closes his eyes, shuddering.

All his openness from earlier, from last night, shuts down. I know a court mask when I see one.

"No."

"Why not?" I press. "I can help you—"

He opens his eyes and glares at me.

"I don't care about the risks," I forge on. "And anyhow, my family does outrank yours. And I can get the king to—"

"No, Valtair."

I search his face, finding pain. Finding determination.

And for a moment we just stare, listening to the sounds of birds in the trees around us, not so many as spring, but not yet quieted for winter.

In the near-distance, someone calls out what sounds

like a greeting in the town. Something bangs. Someone laughs.

The scar on my side pulls when I breathe too deeply.

"I'm dangerous," Morgan says, his voice low and urgent. As if it's of utmost importance that I understand. "My family will not stop looking for me. If they saw me with you—if someone at court recognized me and word got back—" He swallows, and I track the movement. "Maybe your family is more powerful. But mine can still cause trouble. They can still hurt you." He waves at my chest to prove his point.

"Let them try."

"You don't mean that." His eyes search mine. "Your father wants you to marry well. Someone with a title. A family name. Not—" He gestures at himself, his borrowed clothes, the mud on his stolen boots. "Not someone who looks like this. Who'll be seen as a commoner. And I can't be a noble, Valtair. Not and live my own life."

"But wouldn't I be a good match for your family, then?"

"No!" It's a cry of pure despair, and he balls his fists at his sides. His tears are falling anew, and I want to pull him close, wipe them away.

He draws a ragged breath. "I told you. If I'm a man, then I inherit. And my brother doesn't, and that's not in my family's plans. That's not in anyone's plans, I'm supposed to marry as a woman, and forge those ties as a woman, so that my brother's inheritance grows stronger, not—not—" He dashes his sleeve across his eyes, sniffs loudly. "And even if they decide I don't inherit, they'll have to disown me. Or—or I don't know what."

He looks at me with eyes shifting between defiance and pleading.

And I look away. I step back. Because I'm not going to do that to him.

"I could go with you to talk to them," I say quietly, holding out an empty palm. My peace offering. "If you want to tell them who you are, and see if it would turn out better than you think."

"What would your father say in a situation that isn't what he imagined for you?" Morgan snaps back. "Would he just take it nicely, better than you thought?"

"I don't know," I say. But...I do. "Okay...point."

He sighs and leans his head back against the tree trunk, trying to regain his composure.

"I would, though," I say. "Go with you for that. Or go to my father, even."

"Valtair, you don't even know me."

"I know that you know me better than almost anyone," I say. And it's true. Not Torovan, maybe, but... maybe even then.

To be seen is to be known, and no one...just *no one* sees me.

Or Morgan.

I know that.

Morgan reaches out a hand without looking, and I twine my fingers in his.

"You are the best man I've met," he says quietly. His voice sing-songy, trying not to cry again.

I am using every one of the court tricks I know to keep from crying myself. Because if I do, I don't think I'll be able to bear letting him go.

"You too," I say.

He gives me a withering look, and I shrug. But I do mean it.

"I have to find out who I am," he says. "Do you get that?"

He says it like he doesn't matter if I get it, because he's going to do it anyway. And my heart, impossibly, falls more for this man.

Because I've met so few who would stand their ground for who they are.

A crow calls from the trees. Wind rattles dead leaves. The cold seeps through my clothes.

This isn't an argument, it's a goodbye.

I force air into my lungs. Try to think past the ache.

"I know you want to protect me, Valtair, but you can't protect me from needing to find myself, can you? And—and whatever that looks like, it will be what I need."

Morgan licks his lips. "You're not—you're not in love with me."

Like he's trying to convince himself the same.

And maybe I've thought men fools for falling in love after one night, but I understand now, I do.

MORGAN

"Can I kiss you?" he asks. "If this is where we part, can I kiss you to remember? To thank you. I—I want to thank you."

I'm not sure this torment is thanks. I'm not sure if his lips touch mine again that I will have the will to let him go.

Does he understand that I'm protecting him, too? That a heart like his is far more worth protecting than a broken soul like mine?

I nod, not trusting myself to speak.

He wets his lips, steps a little closer, then considers me and carefully leans in.

Does he think I'm that fragile?

Or, is he that fragile?

His lips meet mine.

He's holding back the most of his passion, I know. And I'm not kissing back with mine. Because that flame would quickly become an inferno.

And I know I would never leave his arms again.

But what I said is true—I need to know who I am without the definitions of anyone placed on me.

And right now, I can't take the definition of a lover. I can't be his, and also mine.

I have to know who I am, as a man. As a person.

Because I never have before.

I have to figure out my magic, and my place in the world.

The kiss is over too soon.

He pulls back, hesitates like he wants to lean in again, his eyes studying every detail of my face.

And his face blurs as my own eyes stream again. I cup his cheek, bristly with morning stubble that he hadn't taken the time to shave.

His hand closes over mine, pressing my palm to his cheek.

"When you're done finding yourself," he says, "you know where I am."

"You'll have moved on," I say.

"I won't." He pauses. "I can't promise I won't sleep with any other men in the meantime, I do have needs, you know."

I choke a laugh, shaking my head. "I would never ask."

"But my heart—that will be waiting for you."

If I could pause one moment in my life, and stretch it out, to wrap it around myself like the strongest shield, it would be this one.

I study his face, too.

And will I ever see him again?

It's too much to tell myself no, never.

Even if I know that's safer.

"You might not have to run forever," he says. "We might not have to run."

I nod. Because what else can I do.

And step back first, before my will can betray me.

He hands me his travel bag. Then unhooks a purse from his belt.

"Valtair—"

"Wait, let me take enough to get me back to the palace." He shakes out pure gold coins into his hand.

"Valtair, no—"

Then gives me the rest of the purse.

"I will follow you and hound you until you take this," he says. And I know he means it.

So I take the purse. And the bag. His clothes will be a little big on me, I know.

They are too fancy for me by far.

But if I need a change, if mine get wet, and it will be cold walking across the countryside, and maybe sleeping in the open—

I sling the bag over my shoulder.

And barely get the words out, "Thank you."

He nods.

And then I turn. And I start to walk away.

One step, then the next. And none of them get easier.

I trudge up the hill through the trees, and stop at the top, too weak in my will not to look back.

He hasn't followed me. But he's still watching.

And I see the glint of wet on his cheeks, too.

I turn again before I run back down to him.

And tell myself—six months.

Six months to become man enough to deserve him.

CHAPTER 10

THE GUARD

MORGAN

Five months. It took me five months to be here, with Valtair's traveling bag slung over my shoulder, staring up at the palace gates.

I inhale the sharp morning air, stepping aside as a carriage clatters past me through the open gates. Flexing my fingers inside my leather gloves.

Spring has crept over the kingdom after a hard and bitter winter. And I don't know if there will be any warmth awaiting me here. If I'll have any success to why I've come—and I'm not going to ask for Valtair's help. I'm not.

If he even remembers me.

But...of course he'll remember me. Of course he will.

I nervously adjust the bag's strap again, then walk inside to the bustling palace courtyard.

The guards watch warily. As they should, after the death of their king.

I've heard rumors that King Torovan killed his father the king to assume the throne. But I don't believe them. I only saw Torovan from a distance at the Harvest Festival all those years ago, not long enough to make any kind of judgment on his character.

But, I know Valtair. And Valtair is not the kind of man who would stand by someone who'd kill his father. Of that, I am absolutely sure. And if the king has enemies, he needs allies, too.

My binding garment chafes beneath my shirt and coat, still slightly damp from washing it in the last inn. I did get a proper inn this time, a proper bath and a proper meal. My purse on my belt is heavier than it's been in months, after completing my last caravan guard job.

And I'm *good* at my job. I've learned to take my training growing up and turn it into actual protection, and I've completed two full caravan journeys across the kingdom now.

My clothes are still simple, though they fit properly now, I had enough coin to get them tailored last month. My hair's grown out enough to tie back, and I don't feel the need anymore to chop it short, or fear being called a woman. That happened only once, and early on. It hasn't happened again.

Valtair's clothes—I hadn't wanted to part with them,

but I sold them early to get through that first impossible month.

I've learned how to walk like the man I am, to take up the space I need, to look other men in the eyes. Calluses ridge my palms, and I even have a few battle scars from fighting off bandits.

And I have a letter in my pocket from Lord Ranlen, whose caravan I helped protect through the winter, recommending me to the commander of the palace guard.

The guards working with me in the caravan, they told me that is a guaranteed ticket into the king's guard. And while they wished me all the luck and slapped my back to congratulate me, they didn't wish to be a king's guard, too.

"Too rigid," one had said. "You can't drink at nights like we can on the road."

And another warned it would be dangerous. That I might be working for a king who was more tyrant than king.

But...I don't think so.

In the palace courtyard, I pause only long enough to look up at the towering stone wall above me, with its intricate spires and stonework. I wonder, with a heart-stuttering moment, if Valtair is looking out of any of those windows above, and if he is, would he even recognize me? With my sun-tanned face and cold-wind squint?

My palms sweat despite the cold. I duck my head and continue inside.

In the entry hall, I hold up my letter to one of the palace guards. He gives me a once-over and doesn't come away looking impressed.

He doesn't look at the letter either.

"Commander Ildavan is the garrison commander, he's in the town today—"

"I want to speak with the commander of the king's guard," I press, and I hope it's not too far. But I didn't come here to join the rank and file of the garrison. "I wish to join the king's guard—"

"Then you'll want to talk to Kas," the man says, "and he's busy guarding the king. You'll have to wait in the barracks office until tonight."

It's morning now.

I swallow, but give a firm nod. "And where can I find the barracks office?"

The guard gives me directions, and I make my way through first the glittering part of the palace, then into the service corridors, and finally the palace guard's barracks.

I'm watching every moment for Valtair. But I don't see him.

Is he even in the palace? I met him when he was traveling, and how often does he travel?

The nobles I pass don't even look at me, a random and

obviously common stranger. Or maybe they already assume I'm part of the palace staff.

The secretary of the barracks office points me to a bench and tells me to wait.

So I sit. And I wait.

And I don't rise as the sun slowly shifts in the sky out the office's narrow window. I ignore the growling of my stomach. And only get up to stretch once when there's a cramp in my leg. The office secretary barely glances at me. Do men come in and ask to be palace guards all the time?

Several guards in the green and gold palace livery, with oiled leather armor creaking, come in and out throughout the day. I look up, but no one pays much attention to me.

I'm starting to grow worried that Kas has been in and out and the secretary didn't bother to tell me.

But it's afternoon when a tall, middle-aged man with a rugged, pock-marked brown face steps in. He's dressed in the same green and gold as the other palace guards, his armor slightly scuffed as if he trains in it, too, his dark blue cloak trailing the stone floor. But his bearing has more unconscious command than the others. This is a man used to directing others, and I recognize that immediately.

And stand.

"Are you Kas?" I ask, before the secretary can say anything. Or stop me.

The man pauses near the secretary's desk and turns back to me.

"Yes. What of it?"

"Sir. I have a letter of recommendation to join the king's guard." I hold out the letter I've held clenched in my hands these last hours.

Kas takes the letter with a frown and scans it.

He looks back up to me. "You defended the life of Lord Ranlen's son, against a troop of bandits that included a fire elementalist, when two of the other guards ran?"

I catch my breath. The letter had been sealed, I hadn't yet read it. "Yes, sir. Though, two of the other guards also remained. There had been five of us."

That fight had been desperate, and we got lucky when the snow beneath the bandits' feet turned to ice.

Lucky.

It took me months to figure out how to do that with my elemental magic without anyone else knowing what had happened.

I flex my hand, press it back to my side.

Kas regards me. Then takes a breath. "Lord Ranlen is notoriously picky about who guards his caravans, and who he recommends." He glances to the secretary. "Give Amos here your information, you'll get a place—probationary, mind you—to begin training with the guards. And we'll take your measure."

I swallow. "Thank you, sir. May I speak with you in private?"

It's too much to ask, I know it is. But I told myself —I promised myself—that if I'm going to make my way in the world, I'm not going to do it constantly looking over my shoulder. Constantly being afraid of someone seeing my binding garment. Or dismissing me because of who I am, because I can't take off my shirt, because I can't bathe with the other men. Because I still, despite the herbs I take, which have given me the slightest fuzz of a beard where my magic could not, sometimes bleed.

"Amos, you're due for a break," Kas says, still eyeing me.

The older secretary gets up without a word and shuffles out.

And I do my best, my very best, not to look nervous under Kas's penetrating stare.

"All right, what is it?" he asks.

I straighten my spine, and don't look quite at him.

"I have to tell you that I wasn't born a man. But, I am a man, and an excellent fighter, as my recommendation says. But, I don't want there to be any misunderstandings."

I chance a look, and he's still regarding me, but more thoughtfully this time.

So I venture again, "Sir, I want nothing more than to serve my king."

Slowly, he nods.

"Thank you for informing me. And what did you say your name is?"

I hadn't yet. "Morgan, sir."

"Morgan. All right, then, take your place in the barracks, be at training fourth turn of the glass tomorrow morning. Don't be late."

He hands me back the letter of recommendation. "Send Amos back in on your way out."

I swallow, and blink hard to not let my eyes fill again.

"Thank you, sir."

I hurry out before he can change his mind.

I'M WALKING through the palace corridors after the training session the next morning, wearing the borrowed tunic and basic leather armor the guards gave me. I'm not officially a guard yet, but Kas gave me a nod of approval at my skills today. Reveyan, another of the king's guards, told me to go change and then meet him at the entrance to the royal chambers. To become a palace guard, I have to meet and swear my personal oath to the king.

I'm trying to think through how I'll present myself to King Torovan, when I hear an indrawn breath to my right.

I look over and stop.

Valtair.

He's wearing a light blue coat today, heavy with gold embroidery. His eyelids are shimmered with a light dusting of gold, and his lips part, his eyes widening with shock.

I inhale sharply. It's like the last five months were nothing. It's like we never stepped apart. My body fires itself into a frenzy.

"It's you," he says, almost breathlessly, and walks quickly toward me. He looks around. "What—Morgan, are you here looking for me—"

But he takes in my armor, my borrowed tunic, my sweat from training this morning.

"I'm joining the king's guard," I say. "Um. I'm going to meet Reveyan, one of the guards, to go swear to the king."

"Shit," he says. He looks around us, rubs his hands together, then says, "I'll take you to Torovan. Come on."

His tone is shifting to business. And we're in a more traveled area, palace staff and courtiers tracking through.

Valtair turns with a swish of his knee-length coat, and I follow.

I want to catch up with him, to loop my arm in his, to just...to touch him, to have contact, to make sure our connection is still there.

But he's a high noble in this palace. And I'm about to be a palace guard—effectively invisible.

Which was the other reason I wanted to come. I can help the king, yes, I know I can. But, few nobles in a palace ever truly look at the guards. The guards are just there.

I know my own family will be no exception. They would never think to look for me here.

I follow Valtair up an ornate staircase, and down another corridor, where he stops and waves at two guards on duty. Is this the entrance to the royal quarters?

Reveyan isn't here yet. And I'm still a sweaty mess from training.

But I don't protest. The guards open the doors for us, and Valtair ushers me through. Then stops inside, the door closing again behind us.

The corridor is long, wood-paneled walls lined with oil sconces to keep it mostly bright. Portraits of what must be previous kings line the hall, and there's a quiet hush, a sense of gravity here.

The doors are all closed, and there are no windows. Which one of those doors leads to the king's rooms?

Valtair turns to me and grips my arms. His eyes rake over me, over my face, my body, back up to my eyes.

"Are you well?" he asks.

I nod. "Yes. Well enough."

I search him, too. And I don't like the signs I see on his face of strain. The puffiness under his eyes like he's been getting less sleep. The tight pull of his shoulders.

"Are you?" I ask.

He makes a soft, bitter snort. "Things in the palace have not been...shall we say, easy, after the death of the king." His eyes rake over me again. "But you're here to be a king's guard."

He takes a breath, and steps back. And I want to move forward again, to touch his face, to grip his hands.

I wet my lips.

"I've been a guard for the last months," I say. "Caravans, mostly, a few times guarding nobles personally."

"This isn't what I meant when I said come to the palace. Morgan—the palace isn't safe. Least of all as a guard."

"Then let me help keep it safer."

He makes a frustrated grimace.

And why is he acting like this?

He was willing to cross the countryside with me. He took a dagger to his side—for me.

"I'll be here," I say. "I'm here now."

But I don't know if he's moved on.

And I do know...I'm not the same man who was so desperate for approval that first night together.

I know I carry myself differently now.

Will I think of him differently?

Will he think differently of me?

He seems to be drawing himself up into his noble bearing, and I...I'm just a guard.

I duck my head. "My lord."

He makes a sound deep in his throat and crosses back to me. He tips up my chin.

"No. Never do that. Not when we're alone." His jaw works like he's trying to think if he should say more. But he says, "It's just...it's been a rough few months. It is good to see you. It is *very* good to see you."

His eyes flit to my mouth, back up to my eyes. I see hunger in his own, along with a desperate battle within him.

I'm floating on the edge of hope, on the edge of despair, on the edge of something I can't define.

"And your family?" he asks. "Did they ever find you?"

"No. And they won't here. I am not the person they knew, you know that."

He hesitates. Then slowly tucks my hair back behind my ear. Runs his hand down my cheek.

I shiver, every nerve ending coming awake in a way I haven't felt in all the time since I was last with him.

I watch him, waiting to see what he'll do.

The fire between us is still there, I can see that. I'm almost burning with the need to pull him away, to find somewhere private, to rake my hands down his chest.

To love on every beautiful inch of him.

He pauses again, looks into my eyes.

"Can we take it slow?" he whispers. Almost like he's scared.

My breath hitches.

I feel like I've walked into emotions I don't understand.

I feel like—I feel like we met together once before in our mutual need, in our wine, and now, we've lived our lives between that moment and now. We've filled our lives with different things.

But that need is still there. It's so obviously still there.

But he's holding back.

And I...well, would it even be appropriate for a king's guard to be with a high noble in the king's court? Especially his best friend?

"Slow," I say, and grip his arm as he caresses my cheek again. I lean into the touch.

And then it's me who steps away first.

Because yes, I came here for him. I did. I came for that recognition of souls between us.

I came for the warmth of his body, which I have missed sorely all these months. I've had no one else to warm my bed.

But being a palace guard is important to me.

I *know* I'm good at what I do.

I want to use my body to protect, too, because it's my body to use.

I want to use it here, in this way. This is the life I want to live.

And does that life include this man in the way I want him, too?

Does his life include me?

Can it?

I don't know how I *do* want him. I don't know what he can give.

He's a high noble. And I'm a guard. He knows the fact of my noble birth, but no one else does, and that does matter here. I know that matters to his father.

I'm not a noble anymore.

I take his hand, lower his arm, grip it tightly. "Have you moved on?"

Because I need to know. I do desperately need to know.

"No," he says, breathless again. "No. You?"

"No."

He leans in and, so softly it's barely a touch, brushes his lips against mine.

"Then wait. Please," he says. "Until I sort out what's happening with Torovan and the kingdom. Until I sort out my father, too. And—and my life is a mess, Morgan. You don't know me like you think you do, I'm—I really am a mess. You're—" I hear his swallow. "You're too important for me to fumble into again. I can't mess this up again."

My throat tightens. He didn't mess it up the first time. That had been me, and my own disaster of a life.

But my life isn't a disaster now. I know what I want, and what I want is a few doors down this corridor.

And standing right in front of me.

I lick my lips. "Then, can you wait, too, until I figure out what it means to be a king's guard?"

"You really want this?" he asks.

"I really do."

He kisses me again, more lingering this time.

I hear a sound down the corridor and jump back, whip around, feeling like a teenager caught in a tumble.

But there's no one down the hall—that sound must have come from within one of the rooms.

I inhale the overpowering aura of Valtair's cologne. I've wanted to inhale that scent again for months.

Will being near him be enough? Will I like him the same way in this place where he has to wear his social masks? Where he's bound by his duty to his family and the king?

Will he like me in my place as someone who will keep him safe, and not the other way around? Bound within my own needs and duty?

We met on the road, apart from our daily lives, but we're here now. I saw his compassion, I saw his hurt, I saw his hopes.

But all of those were only a part of him.

And my own were only a part of me.

This...this is where we see the whole of it.

Will we meet in the dark corners of the night, will we wake in each other's arms?

Or will we watch each other from afar, and grow closer, or grow apart?

I gave myself six months to be worthy of him.

I can wait a few months more to find out if we're more than one night's flame.

"Come," he says, tugging my hand, until he lets go. "I'll introduce you to the king."

Thanks so much for reading, and I hope you enjoyed *An Elemental Meeting!*

The story continues in *An Elemental Husband,* out in 2026.

Read my next books as I write them on my Patreon!
https://www.patreon.com/novaecaelum

Want to stay up to date on the latest books? Sign up for my newsletter!
https://novaecaelum.com/pages/newsletter

Acknowledgments

To everyone who read this as I was writing it, who pre-ordered, who cheered this crazy idea to crash write a new novella right at the holidays on, thank you!!

To all my patrons, you are amazing, I love you all dearly! Your support means the world to me!

Huge thanks to Jackie, Ashley, Janet, and Nathaniel, you all are amazing and help keep this all running!

And as always, to my family and friends who've happily cheered me on! You rock! <3

ABOUT THE AUTHOR

Novae Caelum writes romantasy and epic space fantasy with diverse and inclusive main characters.

Novae's pronouns are he/they/starself. He's trans-masc, genderfluid, and ace, and a whole queer galaxy of other things as well.

Novae's fiction has been in Lambda Award-winning and World Fantasy finalist anthologies, and he has short stories archived on the moon!

Novae lives and writes in the American Southwest with his very favorite pup, Major Samantha Carter, who is the cutest.

Standalone

Magnificent: A Nonbinary Superhero Novella

The Throne of Eleven

Lives on Other Worlds

Sky and Dew

Visit Novae Caelum's website to find out where to read these titles direct from the author!

https://novaecaelum.com

9 781958 696583